C
W

DATE DUE

Demco No. 62-0549

Just One Indian Boy

Just One Indian Boy

ELIZABETH WITHERIDGE

Atheneum 1974 New York

*This book is dedicated
to my friends,
Don and Martha,
who inspired it.*

Just One Indian Boy

one

Andy walked down the front steps of the high school at noon, carrying his lunch in a brown paper bag. He would eat it sitting on the grass in the sun while the other students went up to the cafeteria to have a hot lunch; they would have cartons of milk, or maybe some pop to drink, and perhaps ice-cream bars for dessert. They were surging up the steps now, laughing and talking. One of them, paying no attention, not even seeing him, bumped into him.

His brown paper sack fell to the steps and split open. Out of it rolled the greatest delicacy his mother could give him—a baked rabbit head. It began to roll down the steps and bounced clear to the bottom before it stopped. At first Andy stood motionless, too stunned to move, and then he became aware of sound welling up all around him—wave after wave of laughter; hoots, roars, howls, and somehow worst of all, giggles.

"Why don't you pick it up and eat it, Injun?" somebody yelled.

"Yeah, it oughta be real tasty with dirt all over it," somebody else taunted.

"Yuck!" shuddered one of the girls. "What in the world is it?"

Andy started to run down the steps. At the bottom he slowed to swoop up the crisp, brown rabbit head; then he ran on and on, down the walk, through the town, seeing nothing, hearing nothing but the echoes of laughter in his ears. He had no idea of where he was going or what he would do. He couldn't think of anything but this, the latest in the long list of humiliations that had been accumulating the whole two weeks he had spent in high school. It was the end; he knew it was, even though he couldn't think coherently yet. He would never go back again.

He would never return to the gym locker room where his hurt had been the worst of all. There he had stubbornly refused to change his clothes for phys. ed., let alone strip for a shower the way the others did. He couldn't bear to have them know that his mother made him wear long johns in September to save him from the cold that already blew off Lake Vermilion.

At last he came to the railroad track where the silver rails gleamed in the sun as far as he could see. He knew he should follow the track to the lake and the Indian village where he lived. But he couldn't go home again; that decision was made. Everybody would stand around and stare and ask questions, and his mother would look at him sternly and say,

"Andrew, you *must* go back to school! Nothing is as important as your education."

4

She always said that when they argued about school. And they argued often. He seemed to be the only one of his big family who didn't think much of school.

"It isn't that you aren't smart," she would grieve. "If you were dumb, I'd feel sorry for you."

He had kept going only because he was too young to drop out. But now he wasn't going back. He stood still for a minute and looked down the road that led home; he could see his mother in his mind, standing in the door of their house watching for the children to come racing from the bus after school. For a moment he faltered; but then he turned and headed north and east where far down the shining rails he would come to Ely. He didn't know how far Ely was; but he remembered a man from his village who had walked there and hired on in the woods with a logging crew. The man had been gone a year; and when he came home he had fantastic tales to tell of life in the lumber camp and the big money he earned. Nobody ever saw any of the money; but he had said he made it, and Andy believed him.

As he walked down the ties between the rails, his mind began to work again. What would his mother think when the bus brought the other kids back after school and he wasn't with them? Ellen and Rosemary wouldn't know where he had gone or what had happened at lunchtime. He had been alone. Not one living soul would know what had become of him. The teachers wouldn't know, nor the white kids, and he doubted if any people in town would remember seeing an Indian boy walking the tracks toward Ely.

How would his mother find out about him? Would she care terribly? He knew she would. He wondered if she

5

would cry about him. He had never seen her cry; in all his fourteen years he had never seen tears in her eyes. She hadn't even cried when his father went away and left her with all of the kids to take care of. He'd said he would come back, but he never did. If Andy's mother knew what had become of him, she didn't tell the family. She just went on working around the house, doing day work in town so she could get food and clothes for them, fishing summer and winter, and hunting as though she were a man.

She'd take aim at a deer and shoot it slick and clean; and he remembered the day she killed a great black bear rooting around their garbage can—felled it with one shot. She took them all berrying in the summer and ricing over at Nett Lake in the fall. In the winter she skated with them on Lake Vermilion, right out in front of their own house. Somehow, in spite of all she had to do to keep her family from going hungry and dirty, she always had time to have fun with them. Andy turned around and looked back down the track toward home. Once again he faltered, but home was too far behind him now.

If he changed his mind and went home, she would make him go back to school; she would *make* him go. He knew she would. He turned around again and started toward Ely. He would go there and find the place where they hired men for the woods. The man who had told him about it said it was on the main street; it shouldn't be hard to find. Winter wasn't far off—another month and there would be snow, even though he was so hot under the September sun that he had to strip his jacket off. He wasn't sure what a fourteen-year-old boy could do in a lumber camp; but he was big for his age, and strong, and maybe he could pass for sixteen or even seventeen. He would earn a lot of money and buy his mother everything she needed for the house. He kept thinking about that as he hopped from tie to tie, and the thought made running away seem less terrifying.

Andy was in a rush to get as far as he could while it was still light. Once in awhile he had to stop to rest a little. And he got terribly hungry as the afternoon wore on. Worse yet, he got very thirsty; so he was relieved to see the waters of Eagle Nest Lake glittering through the trees at the right of the track. He was sure it was Eagle Nest; he had hiked there once with his older brother. He would stop and wash off his rabbit head and eat it. Thank goodness he had saved that from his lunch at least; the rest of it had probably been trampled all over the steps of the high school. There had been a couple of bannocks and a little sack of popped wild rice, much better than popcorn. Andy's dry mouth managed to water a bit at the thought of it.

He came to the shore of the lake and crawled out on the rocks that lined the edge. He scooped the cool water into his hands and gulped it down. Then he washed his rabbit head and sat down to eat it.

"Why don't you eat it, Injun?"

The words rang again in Andy's ears, but white kids just didn't know how good a baked rabbit head tasted! When he had licked the last vestige from his fingers, he knelt beside the lake again, drank from it and splashed it all over his hot face and neck. His feet were hot, too, and sore. He pulled off his shoes and socks and washed his feet in the cold water. Just as he thought—there was a big blister on one heel; it

7

had broken and started to bleed. The water helped a little. If only he had something to bandage it with, but he didn't even have a handkerchief. He knew he couldn't walk all the rest of the way to Ely in his bare feet; so he put his shoes and socks back on and hobbled off to the railroad track.

The afternoon wore on, still very hot, with his blister hurting more all the time. He was pretty sure he was getting one on the other heel, too, but he didn't want to look. As the sun began to drop toward the edge of the sky, it got cooler, and he would have felt better if it hadn't been for his feet and something frightening that happened.

It must have been almost suppertime when Andy saw what looked like a little town down the track just ahead. As he drew nearer, he saw lights in some of the houses, and a sign on the tiny depot beside the track said ROBINSON. Somehow he felt afraid. If people saw him as he went through, they might try to stop him.

Andy limped along warily, his heart pumping hard, his hands wet and cold. Then he saw to his relief that the tracks didn't really go through the town, but skirted around it. His heart quieted down and he breathed easily again; but as he rounded a little bend, there was a house ahead of him in the dusk. It was very close to the tracks, and he could see a man sitting on the porch, rocking and smoking a pipe. He felt alarm leaping up inside of him again. He thought if he crept along softly as Indians do in the woods, he might not be seen in the twilight; so he crawled past the house, never looking in the man's direction. Just as he thought he had it made, he stepped on a big, sharp cinder. It wrenched his foot and scraped the blister unbearably. Andy let out a little yelp of pain and the man saw him. He got out of his rocking chair and hailed him,

"Hey, young feller, sumpin' happen to ya? Where're ya goin' anyway?"

Andy began to run, blisters and all, which, of course, made the man think he had been stealing or doing *something* wrong. The man began to chase him. Andy didn't dare look back. He could hear the man lumbering along behind him, breathing hard and cursing that "damn Injun" every few steps. By that he knew his pursuer was old and couldn't run very fast. Andy came ahead of him to another little bend in the roadbed, and before he rounded it he slithered off down the steep embankment and huddled in thick brush at the bottom. He lay there panting, nursing the scratches on his hands and arms from the cinders he had slid down on, listening for the old man to go thudding by. He stopped just beyond the place where Andy hid and stood there briefly; then he turned around and walked slowly homeward, muttering as he passed,

"Damn Injun! What become of him? Wonder what he done."

When he was sure the man was safely out of sight, Andy crawled up onto the track and hobbled along more painfully than before. The sun had slipped behind the trees and the stars were coming out. A great harvest moon hung over the track ahead of him, as if it were a beacon put there to light his way. He heard the long, mournful wail of a train whistle and jumped off the track just in time to let it go by on its way to Ely. If only he could have caught a ride on it! He was desperately tired, but he kept going. He had often walked

9

many miles in the woods around his lake when he was hunting or berrying, but there he wore soft deerskin moccasins on his feet instead of the heavy store shoes and the coarse, scratchy socks he had for school.

As he limped along the track, finally the pain was so sharp he hardly knew what he was doing. He wondered numbly if there would be another train along, but he didn't dare leave the track for fear he might get lost in the darkness. Once he thought of lying down somewhere near the track and sleeping the rest of the night, but he was afraid to do that; so he shut off his mind and plodded dumbly along. Time dragged on, and at last he came to Ely. He had no idea what time it was or how many hours it had taken him to get there.

The town was dark, except for the streetlights. There wasn't any light in the depot and even the bars were closed. No one was walking on the streets at all, so he knew it must be very late. He limped along until he came to a small building with a sign he could read by the light on the corner. It said, in bold black letters:

EMPLOYMENT OFFICE

That was the place! He tried the door; it was unlocked, and he crawled into a little entryway. The inside door was bolted, but Andy's bloody feet wouldn't hold him up anymore. He slumped down, pulled his shoes and socks off, and curled up on the floor with his jacket for a pillow. He must have fallen asleep instantly.

two

"Mother of God, what have we got here?"

The sounds barely pierced Andy's consciousness. He struggled out of his deep sleep and peered groggily up into the weatherbeaten brown face of a man bending over him. He was a Chippewa, Andy was sure, and for a minute he thought he was back home on the Lake Vermilion Reservation. He was still too numb to speak, so the man tried again, this time in Ojibway.

"*Ge-do-Ojibway-anah?*"

Andy hesitated, so the man repeated it in English,

"You speak Ojibway, boy?"

"A little bit," Andy said, scraping his blistered heels on the dirty floor as he sat up. The man saw him wince and looked down.

"Mother of God, what have we got here!" he exclaimed again, only this time he was looking at the gory feet. "*Ne-de-a-jib-bah-yan?* You come a long way, boy!"

Andy knew the man wanted to know where he came from.

And he was awake enough now to be wary; he wasn't about to tell anyone where he lived until he knew whom he was talking to. Andy mumbled something; the man pretended to understand and went on talking.

"How old?"

"Sixteen," Andy lied brazenly.

The dark eyes bored down, as if they were trying to examine every inch of him. They took in the rumpled school clothes, the heavy leather shoes, the bloody, coarse-knit socks, and then they returned to his face.

"*Ho-wah!*" was all the man said; but there was a skeptical smile at the corners of his mouth.

"*Ge-bah-ka-day, anah?*" It was more a statement than a question. Andy didn't have to test his knowledge of the Chippewa language much to know that the man was asking if he were hungry. He was starving, and the remark brought him to his feet at once.

"You alone here? Nobody's come to the office yet?" the man asked.

"Nobody, unless I was asleep," Andy answered.

The man stepped around him and tried the inner door. He shook his head and put his arm around Andy's shoulders.

"*Om-bay-o-we-sin-ne-dah,*" he assured him. "*Om-bay.*"

Andy obeyed him and they went out into the street together. He had never been in Ely before—in fact, he had never been farther from home than Nett Lake for the ricing every fall. The noisy café where they went for breakfast seemed like a banquet hall.

They sat on stools at the counter, and the man ordered pancakes and sausages for both of them. The waitress brought coffee for the man and a big glass of milk for Andy. He gulped it down, and when his food came he ate ravenously. The man sat and stirred his coffee and watched silently while the pancakes disappeared. Finally he said,

"My name's Johnny Hawk. What's yours?"

"Andy," he answered shortly, scared to death he would hear, "Andy what?"

But Johnny Hawk didn't ask. He spread butter on his pancakes, poured on some syrup and told the girl to bring more pancakes and another glass of milk for Andy. Johnny chewed on a big bite of sausage and volunteered,

"Nett Lake *ne-doc-gee-bah*."

Andy was appalled to hear that Johnny was from Nett Lake, for the Indian reservation at Nett Lake and the village where he lived on Lake Vermilion were part of the same reservation, called Bois Forte. They were sixty miles apart, but Andy was sure that his new friend would recognize his mother's name instantly. So he changed the subject.

"Shouldn't we hurry and get back to the office to see about my job?"

"Plenty of time to see about your job," Johnny said comfortably. He took another huge bite of pancake, dripping with syrup, and asked another question.

"What do you want a job for? Why aren't you in school?"

"*Gahween!*" Andy shook his head vehemently. It was easy to slip into an Ojibway exclamation when he was aroused. "I'm through with school. I want a job. I want to earn money!"

Johnny looked at him sadly. "You won't earn much money if you don't go to school first."

13

Andy snorted. "I won't earn *any* money unless I get a job," he said bitterly. "I can read and write pretty good and I know enough about figures to get along. What else does an Indian need? In the white man's school I couldn't get any more if I wanted to."

"Let's go back to the office." Johnny sighed, getting up to pay the bill.

"Thanks for the breakfast. I'll pay you back when I get some money," Andy promised.

Johnny tousled his hair and opened the door. "Forget it, *gwe-we-zance,*" he said.

On the way back to the office, Johnny said he was cook for a big lumber outfit that was logging over at Angleworm Lake. He was in town to look for a boy to be cook's helper and dishwasher. The one he had had gone home because his father died, so his boss had sent him into town to find another who suited him. He grinned and asked,

"What kind of job *you* lookin' for, Andy?"

Andy's guard was down. "That's just the kind I want, Johnny," he said. "Would I suit you? Would you take me, *please?* I didn't know if there'd be a place in a lumber camp for anybody—" he hesitated, "my age."

Johnny's eyes began to twinkle.

"Plenty of jobs for sixteen-year-olds, Andy, cuttin' logs. What I need is a *young* feller, thirteen, fourteen, maybe. Hope they got one at the employment office for me. Sure do need a good cookee for winter. What a shame you're too old! I think you and me'd get along good together."

Andy had sprung himself into a trap. And without thinking he blurted it all out, almost as though he couldn't help himself.

"I lied to you, Johnny. I'm only fourteen; honest I am. I ran away from school, but I'm not going back, no matter what you say, or my mother, or anybody else. I hate it—all you get is laughed at and made fun of, and your clothes aren't like the white kids. You start wearing long johns in September, and you don't know half the things they do and," he paused for breath. "Well, anyhow, I'm *not* going back, even if I don't get a job."

"How far did you walk yesterday," Johnny asked.

"From Lake Vermilion," he replied, sheepishly.

"Hmmm, twenty-five miles," Johnny meditated. "Your ma know you quit?"

"Oh no, I just decided to quit and I left right from school," Andy admitted.

"Then your ma don't know what happened. What *did* happen, *gwe-we-zance?*"

Suddenly Andy found himself pouring out the whole tale of the bouncing rabbit head. Johnny listened intently, a frown wrinkling his forehead, nodding every few words.

"I see," he said quietly. "Don't you think your mother is worried about you? Who *is* your mother?"

"My mother is Mary Thunder," Andy told him. Johnny might as well know it all, since he knew so much.

Johnny stopped dead in the middle of the sidewalk and stared at him.

"Mary Thunder of Lake Vermilion!" he exclaimed. "Mary was the prettiest girl I ever knew when we were young. I had hopes for us once, but she married another man instead, and I found me another girl. Her man run off and left her with you young 'uns to raise. I ain't seen her in a dozen years, it must be. I'm always in the woods come ricin' time. She's

15

worried sick about you, Andy. Mary Thunder's a good mother!"

Johnny started walking toward the employment office very fast. Andy had to run to keep up with him.

"All right," he said finally, and there was a new stern note in his voice. "I'll hire you on for my cookee, Andy, but one thing you'll promise me first; you got to send word to her where you are. You hear?"

"Yes, I hear," Andy agreed, "but it won't do any good for her to coax me to go back to school because I'm *not going back!*"

"OK," said Johnny, turning into the employment office to pick up the shoes and socks. "We'll tell Mary Thunder you're through with school—" There was a long pause. "Through with school—for now," he finished, under his breath, but Andy heard.

three

Johnny knew an old Indian in Ely who would be going over to Nett Lake for the ricing in a few days. They went around to see him, and he promised to stop off at the village to tell Andy's mother where he was. Andy didn't know exactly what the old man and Johnny said to each other because they spoke mostly Ojibway, but he felt better.

He even began to feel lighthearted as they went back onto the main street in Ely where Johnny said they must stop to buy him some clothes for the woods.

"You can't cook and wash dishes in *them* things," he said.

"I haven't any money," Andy protested, but Johnny shrugged his broad shoulders and answered casually,

"We'll put it on your bill. You pay me when you get a paycheck."

They began by picking out blue jeans, work shirts, several suits of long johns, and a heavy red-and-black plaid mackinaw.

"Now for mittens and boots," Johnny said, "and plenty socks."

17

Andy looked at his bare feet with the still-raw blisters and wondered if he could ever wear anything on them again. Johnny said they'd be all right if he kept them washed clean and wore moccasins for awhile, so they bought a pair of them, too. Andy had never had so many new things at once in his whole life.

"It will take me a *year* to pay for all this," he objected. It scared him to think of it.

"Have to get 'em all now," Johnny said calmly. "It will be a long time before we come to Ely again."

For the first time Andy began to realize that when the Minnesota winter closed in, he would be shut away from every place and everybody he had ever known. They were in the truck that would carry them out of Ely and miles down Echo Trail to the lake where they would live until spring. Johnny stepped on the starter of the small pickup; it whined and the engine caught. He backed out of the parking place and they were off, down the curving road that wound along beside the lake. Andy looked at the big man sitting beside him and found it hard to believe he had only known him for a couple of hours. He suddenly wondered what would have happened to him without Johnny. What if the employment office man had come first? He had no money, no clothes except the ones on his back, and no friends in Ely. He looked at Johnny again. Johnny must have felt the gaze, for he glanced down at Andy and gave him a friendly slap on the knee.

"What you thinking about, Andy?" he asked.

"About all the stuff you bought for me—breakfast and everything. You don't know me at all. Why did you?" the boy wondered.

Johnny laughed. "I don't know," he said. "Why do *you* think?"

"Maybe you bought clothes for me because you used to know Mary Thunder. But you didn't know she was my mother when you took me to the café for breakfast."

Johnny didn't laugh again. He didn't look at Andy, either; his face was set straight ahead, suddenly grown solemn and grim.

"Once I had a boy like you, Andy," he began. "He was a little older when he quit school, but he had the same story as you. White kids made fun of his clothes, the way he talked, the way he made mistakes. He quit. His mother died about that time. I went back to the woods and stayed all winter, and he was alone. When I come home in the spring, he was gone. They told me he went to the city for a job. No money, no friends, just like you. Nobody to help him. Next time I hear about him, somebody from Nett Lake seen him, drunk on the street at night, just a bum. I went to look for him, but I couldn't find him. That was a long time ago, Andy. I don't know where he is; never hear from him. Maybe he still lives; maybe he's dead."

Andy didn't have the words to tell Johnny how he felt. He just made a sad noise and sat still as they jounced along the road. Johnny was silent, too. At last he sighed and said, with a catch in his voice,

"If he'd had somebody; if he'd had a chance—"

He let the sentence die and gradually the tight lines in his dark face relaxed, and he grinned at Andy again.

"I figure Mary Thunder's *gwe-we-zance* oughta have a chance," he said.

It was fifty miles from Ely to Angleworm Lake. Andy was starving again by the time they turned off Echo Trail onto the dirt road that meandered through the woods. They chugged up to the logging camp—a couple of big buildings and some smaller outbuildings. The first thing Andy saw was the long, tarpaper-covered barracks where Johnny told him the men slept. Next to it was the mess hall, with smoke coming out of the chimney.

"Fred got dinner going, I see," Johnny observed with satisfaction. Fred was the bull cook, Johnny had said. The smell of roasting meat poured from the open door of the mess hall, and just as they were about to go inside, an enormous man came out with a horn and blew a deafening blast that echoed through the words.

"Dinner horn," Johnny explained briefly, steering Andy into the building.

There were several long tables running the length of the hall, and they were covered with food; great platters of beef, bowls of potatoes and other vegetables, trays heaped high with thick slabs of homemade bread. There was a tin plate and cup at each place, and a big wedge of apple pie. Andy looked at all the food and felt almost faint with hunger. Men were beginning to stamp in now and slide into their places. They grabbed bread and forked giant slices of meat onto their plates. He wanted some of it so badly; they never had meat like that at home. He looked at Johnny inquiringly, but Johnny shook his head and said into Andy's ear above the racket,

"Not yet, Andy; it's your job to pour coffee."

Fred came in with his horn, set it down in a corner and

handed him a pot of boiling coffee. He supposed everybody would notice the new cookee, but nobody seemed to. A silence had fallen over the room, broken only by the rattle of the metal dishes, and grunts as the men pointed at food they wanted passed to them. No one thought of anything but eating.

Andy went down the tables pouring coffee. It was steaming hot, and he was scared to death he'd spill some on one of the men. He went back to Fred for more and more; proud and relieved as he neared the end of the last table that he hadn't spilled a drop. Then it happened. He poured coffee for a short, pudgy little man with a red face and a bulbous nose. He reached to set the cup down just as the man unexpectedly shifted on the bench and jiggled Andy's hand. Of course, the hot coffee splashed down onto his lap, and he swung on Andy furiously,

"Doggone dadblasted Injun," he screamed. "Like to scalded me to death!"

Andy had never seen anybody so mad. His first impulse was to turn and rush from the mess hall into the woods where he could hide, but instantly Johnny was at his shoulder. He bent over the enraged man, dabbing at his pants with a wet towel.

"Too bad you got burned," he said soothingly. "Our cookee is new today. He'll do better soon."

"He'll do better," howled the little man, "or I'll run him out of this camp so fast he won't know what hit him."

He kept slapping at his pants and glaring at Andy.

"One more mistake like that and you're a goner."

At any other time Andy would have found the episode

funny, and he half expected the other men to laugh, but no-body did. Andy's hand was shaking so that he could hardly pour the last few cups. Soon after the men began to leave the mess hall in small groups, talking and picking their teeth. And in a little while Johnny, Fred and Andy sat down to eat their own dinner, but Andy was still too upset to enjoy it.

"Why did you say, 'He'll do better soon?' to that man?" Andy demanded resentfully. "It was his own fault. He reared up just as I was putting his cup down."

"I know," Johnny said apologetically. "I saw what hap-pened; but that man is known as Bad Bill, and good reason for it, too. He's got a gosh-awful temper. You have to rub him the right way or you'll get hurt. I sure hope you learned your lesson about him today."

It didn't take Andy long to learn the routine of his job as cookee, and Johnny said he did it well, but he found it a lonely life. There were only a couple of Indians beside Johnny in camp, and no other boys his age at all. There were some men under twenty, but all of them were white and worked in the woods cutting or skidding logs. None of them paid any attention to Andy. Johnny was always his friend, of course, but Johnny was old. Andy had the feeling, too, that Johnny felt the way Indian men always did about the young males in their tribes; he wanted Andy to grow up to be strong and independent. He believed that too much coddling was bad for boys.

Most of the time he let Andy work out his own problems. Andy appreciated this, but he was often lonely. The time Johnny's concern for him showed most was when Andy had a run-in with Bad Bill, and that was often. Bill did not forget nor forgive the coffee incident on Andy's first day. No matter how hard Andy tried to stay away from him, or please him if he did have to serve him, those bloodshot eyes seemed to follow him. Andy decided Bad Bill thoroughly hated him, and Andy heartily hated him back.

four

Andy's mother wrote to him soon after the old Indian from Ely stopped to tell her where he was. He kept her letter tucked under the mattress in his bunk. If she was angry because he had run away, she didn't say so. She wrote about what was going on at home and what his friends were doing. She said they missed him and hoped he was happy in the woods, and saving his money. Her disappointment at his dropping out of school she kept hidden within herself, but he could feel it like a living thing in the letter. It was cold at Lake Vermilion, she said, and she hoped he had warm enough clothes for the woods. There had been ice on the lake the morning she wrote the letter.

There was ice on Angleworm Lake, too, early in the mornings before the sun had time to get at it. Soon the day would come when the sun wouldn't be warm enough to melt it anymore, and then the water would be ice for the rest of the winter. It was nothing for the temperature to drop far below zero in the Minnesota northland—20, 30, 40 below in the dead of winter. Soon he would have to wear the plaid mackinaw and the long johns Johnny had bought for him in Ely. He was already wearing the flannel shirts and the boots, and he answered his mother's letter to reassure her about his new warm clothes.

The hardest job Andy had to do was to carry in wood for the cookstove and the great cast-iron heating stove in the mess hall. He never counted how many armfuls it took every day to feed the roaring monsters, as winter came relentlessly on and bitter winds blew down from the north or off the Dakota prairies. Luckily the men stacked the wood up against the building where he didn't have far to go to get it. Fred often entertained him with stories about his own boyhood when he was a cookee for an outfit over on Burntside Lake near Ely and he had to chop a hole in the ice every day and carry water for the kitchen no matter how cold it was. When it was 40 below, sometimes the hole would freeze over before he got his bucket emptied and raced back for another, he said. Andy privately questioned that part of the story; but he was thankful for the deep well and the electric motor to pump the water into the mess hall!

Andy's work was harder when the cold and snow came, but he liked the long evenings when the men would sit around the stove after supper and swap yarns, which he could hear over the clatter of his dishwashing. The ones he remembered best were the ones they told during the three-day blizzard in February. It began to snow late on a Friday afternoon and didn't stop until sundown on Monday. The men all came in from the woods before the storm got really wild; and a good thing it was, too, for they never could have found their way an hour later.

The blizzard blew in from the north, the worst one Andy

25

had ever seen; before supper was over he couldn't see the bunkhouse, just a few yards away. Some men took a rope and strung it between the two buildings so they would have something to hang onto when it was bedtime. Andy and Johnny went out together to bring in more wood. Johnny wouldn't let him go alone for fear he'd get lost in the snow. They held their bodies against the building as they went around the corner, so they wouldn't wander off and freeze to death in the blizzard. It was so bad that when they went in with the first load, the wind almost blew the door off its hinges, and Johnny called for more men to lend a hand with the wood. He was afraid they couldn't get out in the morning for more.

At bedtime the men decided not to leave the mess hall even though they had strung the rope to the bunkhouse.

"Better stay where the grub is," Johnny said laughing.

In the morning the snow was over the windows, and the doors were sealed shut with the drifts. Three days and three nights it snowed; when it was done the drifts were up to the eaves of the low buildings, and it took the better part of another day for the men to shovel out so the doors could be opened. By that time all the stories had been told. Andy had heard at least a dozen versions of the famous Armistice Day blizzard of 1940, and knew about every other blizzard, cloudburst and tornado anybody could remember or dream up.

One of the men had a mouth organ, so he played, and they all sang songs of the lumber camps and the wars, and finally wound up with gospel choruses. A few decks of playing cards had been found, and games went on at the long tables. On Monday afternoon just as the storm began to wane, two or three fights broke out because everyone was utterly bored. Andy was treated to the fearsome sight of Bad Bill, purple with rage, taking on a man twice his size. Bad Bill knocked the man down, too, and a dozen men rushed to pull him away. Andy wondered what would have happened if someone hadn't yelled just then that the snow had stopped, and even Bill's attention was distracted.

There wasn't much more snow that winter, fortunately, because the drifts they had didn't melt until the end of April; and there were still piles of dirty snow around on Memorial Day when the buds were all bursting on the trees and the woods were full of wildflowers.

By the time spring came, Andy was through paying off his debt to Johnny, and in addition to his job as cookee he was doing some work in the woods. He was delighted when the foreman told him they were a little shorthanded and asked him if he'd like to put in more hours and get more money. Now he would begin to earn that fortune the man from his village had bragged about. When the season was over in the summer and the logs were trucked over to the sawmill, he would go home to his mother with his pockets full of money and she would be glad that he had quit school and gone into the woods.

So he dreamed about his great new money while he skidded logs in the woods. Paydays came and went, and he looked in vain for the money he knew he should be earning. To be sure, his paychecks were larger because he was working longer hours, but it wasn't enough. He understood figures well enough to realize that he was being paid at the same rate for his logging work as he was for washing

27

dishes, waiting table, carrying wood and doing all the other menial jobs he did for Johnny and Fred. It wasn't fair; loggers were paid at a much higher rate than kitchen help. They couldn't fool him about that.

He was disappointed and puzzled and angry, so finally he went to Johnny about it. He showed him his last paycheck and said,

"Johnny, why shouldn't I be earning as much money for my logging as any of the other kids here? I'm doing the same work, and the foreman told me I was doing all right. I'm fifteen now. What's going on?"

Johnny was sitting out on the steps of the mess hall after the supper work was cleared away, smoking his pipe. The smoke drifted on the soft May breeze, and he tapped the pipe on the wooden step and started to refill it before he answered. He lit it again and began to draw slowly on it, staring off over Andy's head into the dusky woods. Then he turned and looked at him.

"Want the truth?" he asked.

"Sure," Andy nodded.

"All right," Johnny said, looking straight at him. "This is it. Two short words . . . you're Indian."

"I'm Indian? Of course I'm Indian, and proud of it!" Andy exclaimed. "What's that got to do with my paycheck being smaller than it should be?"

"Plenty," Johnny answered grimly. "I found out, a long time ago. That's why I cook instead of logging. Why should I log on cook's pay? Stupid!"

Andy jumped up and paced up and down, hot all over with anger as he began to understand what Johnny was driving at.

"You mean to sit there and tell me that I won't ever be paid for logging at the same rate as a white man because I'm an Indian?" he demanded. "That's wrong. It isn't fair. I'm not going to stand for it! I'm going to complain!"

"You'll stand for it or you'll quit lumber camp," Johnny said calmly, sucking on his pipe again. "Times are better than when I was a kid, but your pay still is not as good as a white man's. That's the way it is, boy."

Andy stared at Johnny's impassive face for a long time and could see no real anger in his expression. Instead he had a kind of accepting look, hard to understand. Johnny wasn't stupid; in fact Andy thought he was very intelligent. How had he come to be reconciled to such treatment?

"I'll find out, all right," Andy shouted, "but not the way you mean. I'll find out *why* and I'll do something about it!"

He turned from Johnny and rushed down the trail into the woods, furious and disillusioned. He followed the trail blindly, paying no heed to where he was going, until he suddenly pulled up short on the edge of one of Angleworm Lake's many curves. He stood on the shore in the twilight, looking at the dark blue water, tinged with sunset pink and gold. Standing there, watching the slender ribbon of lake winding its way through the thick woods, Andy felt his anger slowly cooling, and he sat down on a flat rock to think about the two short words Johnny had given him. "You're Indian," he had said, not in anger but in a disturbing, accepting manner.

Were all Indians the same? Or was it perhaps only his own tribe, the Chippewas? Maybe only they were meek and docile, letting white people walk all over them like doormats. Maybe the Navajos and Sioux and Iroquois and Winnebagos and Apaches and all the others were stronger and more willing to stand up for their own rights.

He certainly didn't feel submissive himself. All his humiliation in the high school came flooding back. He recalled the way the white boys at camp had snubbed him, and the mean, petty things that Bad Bill had done all winter to make him mad. Whenever he had to speak to Andy he always called him "you dadblasted Injun!" Andy sat on, brooding, as the sunset colors faded from the water and the stars began to fleck the sky. Suddenly the moon floated up over the blackness of the forest. Andy looked around at the beauty of the spring night, there in that land that had once belonged to his people, and almost without knowing what he was doing he said out loud in the deep stillness,

"This is my own, my native land. . . ."

He couldn't believe he had said those words, part of a poem he had had to learn in school when he was little. When they had to drone them out together he used to say to himself, "How dumb!" But now all alone in the velvet dark, he knew what they meant. He didn't even remember the name of the poet, but he supposed he was a white man, writing those lines to celebrate the land he thought belonged to *his* people. But it didn't. This land belonged to Andy Thunder. It belonged to his people.

A great wave of homesickness flooded over him, and he jumped up and started back to the trail. He would go home to his mother as he had planned, even without all the money he had planned to take to her. He would go as soon as he could get away from camp, as soon as the crew broke up for the summer. He might even run away, right then. But then he realized he couldn't; he couldn't do that to Johnny. Besides he knew now that it was useless to run away—you never left anything behind. You thought you did, but when you turned around, there it was on your heels again.

He would finish his work in the woods, catch a ride into Ely and then he'd walk home along the tracks, the way he had come ten months ago. He would walk home again.

His mind was so full of the future that he didn't look where he was going and suddenly in the darkness of the woods he fell over something. He struggled to his feet, rigid with fear, because the thing he had stumbled on came to life and began to spew forth the worst curses he had ever heard. In the faint moonlight that filtered through the trees he could see that it was a man, and by the sound of the voice he knew it was Bad Bill, and he also knew the man had been drinking. There was a drunken slur to his words, and he was sprawled on the ground, fumbling for something in the dark.

Andy began to run along the path toward camp, and as he turned to look back he caught a glimpse of something glimmering in the pale light as Bad Bill held it triumphantly aloft. He supposed it was a whiskey bottle.

"I got it, you dadblasted Injun," he bellowed, "and if you ever rat on me, I'll kill you. D'you hear me? I'll kill you, I tell you!"

Andy decided Bill must have fallen into a drunken stupor then, because there was a groan and then stillness. He didn't take time to look. All he could think of was getting back to camp; he was scared to death.

31

five

Somebody else must have ratted on Bad Bill, though, because only a few days later the rumor went around camp that he had been fired. The story was told under the breath, but with great satisfaction, because everyone hated and feared him. Andy was in a panic. He tried every way he could think of to keep out of the man's sight, but Bill found him. Andy was coming cautiously around the corner of the mess hall with his arms full of wood when Bill, ready to leave, saw him. The man attacked with the swiftness and ferocity of a wild animal closing in on its prey. The wood flew in all directions, and before Andy could scream for help and run, Bad Bill had him flat on his back with his huge hands around his throat. Bill's furious little bloodshot eyes bored down, until Andy let out one shriek of pure terror, "Johnny!" Then everything went black, and he lost all memory of what happened.

He heard later that Johnny was there in an instant. He clawed at Bad Bill's hands and tore them from Andy's throat with superhuman strength while he shouted for help. Luckily for Andy, the men were straggling out of the woods for dinner and got to him in time, because Johnny could never have held out against Bill. Only the youngest and strongest in camp were a match for him. Three men leaped on him and hurled him to the ground, but the three of them were barely able to control him. Andy was told about the fight afterward and very vaguely remembered hearing the racket.

Finally Bad Bill wrested himself loose from the men, snatched up his duffel bag and lumbered down the road, shouting threats over his shoulder, most of them aimed at Andy. Somebody brought him to with a dipperful of cold water in the face, so he sat up in time to hear Bad Bill yell,

"I'll get you yet, you dadblasted Injun. You'll learn not to rat on me!"

Andy didn't have much time to brood over Bad Bill's attack or nurse the bruises Bill's hands had left on his throat. The next two weeks were busier than all the rest of the year put together. They were spent loading logs onto trucks to be taken to the sawmill, and cleaning up camp ready to close it for the summer. Finally the work was all done, and the time had come to go. Andy's long hitch in the woods was over. He tied his few possessions into a snug bundle and climbed into a car with Johnny and several other men for the ride to Ely. He would leave them there and walk the tracks again to Lake Vermilion. It might take him two days to walk to the Indian village, but he would get there, and he would never again return to the woods and the camp where the red man worked beside the white man for less money.

The man who was taking them to Ely was going on over

to Orr, where the road to Nett Lake Indian Reservation began, so Johnny would ride that far with him. Andy would have to say goodbye to him in Ely, the first man he had really loved in his whole life. He hated that part of going home and hoped that at the last minute Johnny would decide to drop off with him and go to the village to see Mary Thunder. As they neared Ely, he gathered the courage to ask him, but Johnny smiled and shook his head,

"I'd better go home now, Andy. I've been away a long time. I'll see you again someday—maybe you'll come to Nett Lake to rice this fall and bring your ma with you."

They came to Ely and stopped at the café where Johnny had bought his breakfast that morning they had met.

"*Om-bay,* Andy," Johnny said. "I'll buy you lunch."

"Oh no," Andy answered firmly, "this time I am buying lunch for *you. Om-bay!*"

Some of the men from camp were there eating, and they all sat together. When they found out where Andy was going, one of them said,

"I'm going through your town, Andy. Ride with me."

Andy began to shake his head. He wanted to walk home again; to go home the same way he had come. He didn't know why he felt that way about it. It just seemed right. He would stop at a resort he knew across the bay from his village and ask his friend, the Major, if he could borrow a boat for the end of the trip. He would row up to their landing, and the family would come running down to see who had come. What a surprise for his mother! He could hear her now calling,

"Andy, Andy! Where did you come from?"

34

He snapped awake from his daydream to see Johnny staring down at his feet with a big, wide grin on his face.

"Remember those blisters, Andy?" he asked. "You better ride with Mike."

Andy had not forgotten those blisters. He was much tougher now after his winter in the woods, but he suddenly realized the distance all the way home would be farther than the hike he had taken from school. Mike was waiting for his answer, so he nodded reluctantly; and after he had proudly paid the check for his lunch and Johnny's, he shook hands with Johnny and followed Mike out to his car.

They drove through his land, alive now with the green of woods and the flowers of early summer. They passed the road to Eagle Nest Lake where he had washed his bleeding feet, and came at last to his town, across the bay from home.

"I'll leave you here, Mike," Andy decided hastily, although he knew Mike was going on past the turnoff to the Major's place. He thought he could afford a little walk when he was so near home. He thanked Mike for the ride and walked down the sidewalk past the familiar stores and the post office until he came to East Two River where it ran up into the land from the lake. People kept their power boats there, and sometimes in the past he had caught a ride out onto Lake Vermilion. If he could, it would be quicker than going to the Major's. Now that he was so close, he couldn't wait to get home. He walked along the edge of the little river, shored up with old rotting timbers. Lumberjacks had floated logs down this way to the lake and sawmill long ago, but now the swampy shores were lined with boathouses where white people stored their fancy runabouts and cruisers. It would be great if someone he knew came along and offered him a ride across the lake, but nobody seemed to be around; so he walked along until he came to the ruins of the old brick mill, and looming beside it the enormous, abandoned incinerator where waste lumber and sawdust used to be burned in the old days.

That towering shaft of sheet iron was a famous landmark. No matter where you were in a boat on Pike Bay or Big Bay or any of the dozens of inlets and bays of Lake Vermilion, you could always see the gigantic, rusting tower soaring up into the sky and you could find your way home. That part of it was good; but it was also such a vast, forbidding thing, that children on the lake used to think of it as a kind of cast-iron boogeyman. When Andy was little, he had sometimes gone to play around it with his older brothers and sisters. He could still remember shivering with fear when he thought of being shut up in it. Once his biggest brother had threatened to throw him in if he didn't behave.

Now it looked almost friendly, silhouetted against the blue sky of early summer. Andy walked all around it for old times' sake and then went down to the shore where the waves licked at the narrow sand. He stood there wrapped in a stillness so deep he could hear the small ripples licking at the piling far out from shore, and the lowing of a cow on the farm up West Two River. He looked across the lake and could glimpse the houses of his village, and even see his own, down near the shore. He could see children, tiny as dolls, racing around on the hillside, and when he held his breath, he thought he could hear them yelling.

He cupped his hands around his mouth and yelled at them,

but his yells came bouncing back to him across the water. There were no other sounds in the silence of the afternoon— no power boats roaring down Pike Bay, no summer people water-skiing, no fishermen trolling slowly around Whisky Island. He began to wonder how he would get across the lake to his village. Maybe he would have to walk all the way back up the river into town and down the highway to the Major's place after all. He walked along the shore a little way, kicking at a dead fish now and then and trying to decide what to do.

Upside down in the grass a little way up from the shore, he came upon an old rowboat. It had been there for years and years; he remembered seeing it when they had come to play around the tower, and nobody ever saw its owner rowing it or even knew whose it was. He looked at it carefully to spot any break in the bottom, but it seemed to be whole in spite of its age. He began to feel excitement welling up inside of him. He didn't suppose there were any oars around, but he'd turn the old boat over and have a look at it anyhow. It would probably leak like a sieve if he put it into the water—it was so old and dry. But wouldn't it be great to go rowing across the lake and up to their rickety little dock, and there would be his mother, Mary Thunder!

Andy pulled up one side of the boat and gave it a mighty heave. It teetered on its side for a second, then rolled over. Underneath it were a pair of oars, ancient, rotten-looking oars, but *oars*. Andy couldn't believe his eyes. He didn't know whether or not he could possibly row across the bay with them, but all of a sudden he decided to try. He dragged the boat down to the water and shoved it in. The cold brown water began to pour through the cracks between the boards, and he thought he couldn't stand the disappointment. If he'd been a little younger, he'd certainly have cried.

As he stood watching it, however, he noticed that the water level had stopped rising. Andy bent close to examine the floorboards and discovered that they were beginning to swell with the water. Maybe, just maybe a miracle would happen and the boat would turn out to be seaworthy after all! He looked around for something to bail with and found an old coffee can in the grass. He took off his shoes and socks and went to work. It took a long time to get the water all out. Finally it was quite dry; he tossed his bundle of clothes and his shoes and socks aboard, fitted the old oars into the rusty oarlocks, and pushed off from shore. He felt fairly safe about the boat, but the oars were still a question. He had taken a long, sturdy stick into the boat as a precaution; if the oars gave out he could probably pole his way around the shore to the Major's, once he had gotten across that arm of Pike Bay where East and West Two River emptied into the lake. He dipped the oars gingerly into the water and pulled gently. The old boat moved out from shore and nothing bad happened. He turned her nose into the river channels, watching apprehensively for deadheads.

Andy pulled carefully on the oars, moving steadily into deeper water, but all was well. The oars seemed strong enough, so he began to pull a little harder. He was getting out into the widest part of Pike Bay now; he had to decide whether to go on to Whisky Island, which was about half-way between the Indian village and the Major's place, or to take the safer course and go around the shore in shallower water and ask the Major to take him home.

The lake was unusually quiet—no choppy waves. The old boat moved through the water as though she were glad to be in it again. A few white gulls followed him, the oars squeaked in the rusty locks, there was no other sound. He decided to try for Whisky Island. It seemed forever that he rowed the heavy old hulk across the water. But once at the island, he rowed carefully around the rocky shoreline, and headed for the small cove where his village was. No need to go to the Major's now. He'd be home in a little while if all went well. Soon he knew he was close to shallow water and was so near the village that he could really hear the children shouting this time. Some of them had spotted the strange boat heading in toward the shore and had run down to the dock. That, of course, had to be the moment he caught the left oar between two rocks under the water. He had been careless, watching the children, and dipped too deep. He heard a sharp crack, and the blade broke from the oar. He took his stick and poled the rest of the way. The copper-brown faces of the children grew more distinct. He recognized his young brother, Harry, and Ellen and Rosemary, his little sisters. He waved and shouted, and Harry went tearing up the hill to their house screaming,

"Ma! Ma! Andy's here!"

His dream was coming true. The door of his house flew open, and his mother came flying down the path, her arms spread wide. He poled the boat up to the dock and took a flying leap onto the shore and into them. Finally he drew back and looked into her face, and for the first time in his life he saw Mary Thunder's eyes full of tears.

39

six

The first few weeks of that summer were just like one long, beautiful holiday. It was heaven not to have to lug in wood and wash dishes for a crowd of men. Mother cooked everything he liked best and had missed in the woods. She popped wild rice for him, and there were bannocks every day and now and then a baked rabbit head. When the rest of the children complained because they wanted baked rabbit head, too, his mother would say, "Now, now, Andy has been away a long time, and they don't have rabbit heads to eat in the lumber camps."

One morning, though, he awoke early, feeling wrong. He couldn't put his finger on any special thing, but the day was just wrong. The weather was perfect; the lake was a great shining stretch of mirror in front of the village. In the afternoon the water would have warmed enough for swimming, and if he hurried out before the sun was up too high he could probably catch some fish. He heard the drone of a fisherman's boat as he trolled around the rocky shore of Whisky Island.

Andy's old boat was ready to go. He had patched up a leaky spot or two, and an old Indian who lived up the hill had helped him carve out a pair of new oars for her. They even carved fancy knobs on the ends. Sometimes the man did a little carpentry and painting for summer people around the point from the village, so he had little dabs of colored paint left over from his various jobs. He gave the cans to Andy, who painted gorgeous stripes of brilliant colors all around the boat, more to save the wood from rotting than to be decorative. Everybody thought it was magnificent, and Mother told them the Bible story of Joseph's coat of many colors. So they named her *Josie's Coat,* because boats are always female for some reason or other.

With *Josie's Coat* always ready, Andy could dig some angleworms and row out to catch some perch or crappies, maybe, or even a walleye if he were lucky. But that morning he didn't feel lucky; he doubted if he'd even catch an undersized perch if he went. Andy rolled out of bed, threw on some jeans and an old shirt and went down to the water where *Josie* was wallowing gently at the dock. Even the pure lake air and the bright morning didn't help. He didn't feel like fishing. As a matter of fact, he didn't feel like doing anything. He wasn't tired and he wasn't sick; he simply felt lousy.

Dan Upwind started his wheezy old car and headed out of the reservation for his job in town. Suddenly Andy realized he needed something to do. He decided that he needed a regular job with a paycheck at the end of the week—swimming, fishing, loafing and stuffing himself on his mother's cooking weren't enough.

Maybe Dan could find him a job where he worked, but

Andy doubted it. He had often heard the men talking about how hard it was for Indians to get hired. Besides, he was only fifteen and you had to be sixteen to get a full-time job with any kind of good wages. He'd row over to the Major's after breakfast and see if he could work there during the summer. Resort owners needed dock boys and guys to do odd jobs around their places during the season. The day began to look better. He went in to eat breakfast and have some coffee before he set out. His mother thought it was a good idea to *try* for something to do, but he could see she was dubious about his getting a job. She kept shaking her head and saying,

"Go ahead and try, Andy, but don't be too disappointed if you don't get anything."

She had met the Major's wife in town and heard that Bob was coming home for the summer, so he would probably be doing most of the work around their place. At least that was what Mother thought. She followed him down to the dock and watched him push the boat out into the lake. He could see that she was troubled and depressed because he wanted a job.

Andy kept thinking about that, rowing across the water. It seemed a strange reaction from his mother, and it didn't make sense to him. He thought about Johnny, too, and about that peculiar "accepting" look on Johnny's face when they talked about job discrimination at camp. Andy didn't understand that, either. Probably he was too young to understand all that was involved, but he was old enough to know that both his mother and Johnny had been touched by this evil thing. Maybe they had tried to fight it when they were young, but at last they had been beaten down by it. Now his mother wanted to protect him from it, not by fighting, but by avoiding it. Had she acted this way when his older brothers and sisters had entered the white man's world? He had been too young then to notice or understand.

Well, he wasn't going to run away from it. He was going to lick it if he had to fight until the day he died! He pulled hard on the oars, and *Josie* actually took a sluggish leap forward. He had a good visit with the Major. Mother had been right; his son, Bob, was home and would spend the summer working at the boatyard and doing odd jobs around the small resort. So there would be nothing for Andy to do. He knew the Major was sorry; they had always been good friends.

He came down to the lake with Andy to have a look at the boat and told him that it had been abandoned over by the tower as long as he could remember, so he didn't see why Andy shouldn't have it. Whoever had owned it originally must have gone away. He looked her over and complimented Andy on the way he had patched her up, and laughed at the paint job. He agreed that *Josie's Coat* was the perfect name for her.

Andy went home feeling pretty good, in spite of not getting a job. It was great to see how everyone liked his boat; she really seemed like his own boat now, not just a temporary borrowed thing. However, that was the one good thing in what turned out to be a very discouraging time. Johnny and his mother had both been right. It was next to impossible for an Indian teenager to find a job and keep it. He started out by going to several other resorts near their end of the lake. Nobody needed a dock boy or a handyman, at least not a fifteen-year-old Indian handyman. One day he went into town with Dan Upwind and walked up and down the main street looking for a job. When he went home that night, he felt really beat. He was tired, he was discouraged and he needed money.

He had given his mother almost all of the money he had brought home from the lumber camp. She had gone into town one day and bought herself a pretty flowered summer dress because he insisted she spend it for herself instead of on the kids. But after that she never used a cent of it as far as Andy knew. She must have put it away; he didn't ask her because you didn't ask Mary Thunder private things like that. But anyway, he didn't have any money, and he needed some. He'd learned to smoke at camp, and he wanted cigarettes; he certainly couldn't ask Mother for cigarette money and money for candy bars and a show. He was too old for that.

Finally Andy began making the rounds of the summer places at the point every day, asking for odd jobs. Sometimes he got one and earned a dollar or two mowing the grass around a cabin or bailing water out of a boat after rain, or even baby-sitting for a couple of hours while the missus went into town shopping. He didn't make much money, but at least it kept him in cigarettes.

His mother said little about his hunger for a job, but she did bring up a subject he would have been glad to avoid. She had found out soon after his return what had happened to make him run away from school. He decided to tell her the whole miserable story, and of course he wound up with the tale of the bouncing rabbit head. He really thought he told it all very dramatically and in a way sure to get her sympathy.

It didn't work. She was sorry about his problems with the teachers, and the kids laughing at him and calling him Injun, and his trouble wearing long johns and refusing to take showers in the gym. She was even quite indignant about the rabbit head. But she didn't change her mind about school, as he had hoped she would. She sat quietly when he finished, then finally said,

"Andy, I have never known you to be so stupid about anything before. When you had all this trouble in school, why didn't you tell me about it? I would have gone to school and tried to straighten it out with your teachers and the principal. Something could have been done. Now you have lost a whole year of school, and you will have to learn how to study all over again."

Andy decided to take the bull by the horns.

"Don't worry about my losing a year of school, Mother," he reassured her. "It won't make any difference at all."

His mother fixed him with her piercing black gaze and said, "Why?"

"Well," he said, drawing a deep breath, "I have made up my mind not to go back to school this fall."

He hoped the announcement sounded bold and assured. He had never spoken to Mary Thunder like that before, and he felt like jelly inside.

"Oh?" said his mother. Then she just sat and waited for Andy to go on.

After awhile he had to go on, even though there wasn't much else to say.

"There would be no point in my going back to that white kids' school," he said sullenly. "I can't learn anything there."

"Maybe not," his mother said dryly, "but it's the best we can do for you. You know very well I don't have the money to send you off to an Indian boarding school. You weren't a

45

good enough student to get a scholarship like the rest of the family. You didn't work in school."

"But you don't seem to understand, Mother," Andy argued, determined not to back down. "I'm not going back to school again, no matter what you think."

His mother didn't answer that. But a variety of emotions swept over her face. Fury at first, then sadness, and finally she asked,

"What does Johnny think about your going to school?"

"Well, he thinks I should," Andy had to admit.

His mother nodded. "I knew he would," she said. "When he was young I remember how bad he wanted to go to high school, but there was no money, so he had to go to work instead. I was still in school, and one day he said to me, 'You go to school just as long as you can, Mary.' So I would expect him to give my son the same advice. I wish I'd taken it from him then, but I quit to get married. *You* take it, Andy. I found out too late how good his advice was."

"Johnny's smart, all right," Andy agreed, "but I don't believe either of you knows how I hate school."

His mother's tone changed. "There'll be no truant officer coming out here after a son of mine," she said sternly. "You'll go to school until you're sixteen, because that's the law, whether you hate it or not, it makes no difference."

"Oh, Ma," he cried, "how silly! They don't pick up Indian kids. They couldn't care less whether we go to school or not."

Mary Thunder went toward the house to begin supper preparations.

"We'll discuss this another time, Andrew," she threw back over her shoulder.

seven

It wasn't long after Andy's talk with his mother that he met Kenny. Kenny's grandmother lived in the village and everybody liked her. She lived all alone in a terribly ramshackle tarpaper shack and it was hard for her to do things for herself because she was old and crippled with arthritis. Andy's mother often took hot, fresh bannocks to her when she was frying them for the family. One day she came home from Granny Kingfisher's with news.

"You can't imagine what good luck for Granny!" she exclaimed, dropping more batter in the hot grease. "Her daughter Rose's boy, Kenny, is coming to spend the summer with her. She's so happy. He can carry her water, shop for groceries and do the chores around the place. Maybe he'll even fix it up a little if he's handy. I never saw such a mess as that shack is in. Poor dear old soul, she can't do a thing for herself anymore."

Mother sighed and fished the bannocks out of the smoking fat. Andy had been sitting idly by bored, waiting for his sup-

47

per. Suddenly he perked up. Maybe the summer wouldn't be so bad after all, with a boy from the city here. His young brother Harry wasn't too much company for him.

"How old is he?" Andy asked. "Would he be somebody for me to hang around with?"

"I 'spose so," she answered. "Let's see. Kenny must be seventeen or eighteen by now. He was born while Rosy and her husband still lived here, and they've been gone a long time. Come to think of it, he was born the same year your brother Peter was. He must be eighteen this summer. You're a little young for him, but with the older boys away he just might take to you."

Kenny arrived a few days later, and he did take to Andy, probably because Andy was closer to his age than anyone else around. Not many Indian kids stayed on the reservation, once they were sixteen. Andy's older brothers were working with a construction gang out in the western part of the state that summer, earning college money for the next year. Some of the other young guys were in college or working but most of them had gone to the cities, looking for jobs. Almost none ever came back to live. Granny Kingfisher loved to talk about the old days when there was a big Indian boarding school on the shores of Lake Vermilion, with hundreds of Indians living in the village. Now it had dwindled to only fifty or sixty people and the school was gone, its buildings torn down and only the ruins of a barn left as a reminder that it had ever been there. Andy found it lonesome so he was glad that a new boy had come, even though Kenny did boast too much about life in the city.

Andy learned a lot about Kenny and his life, from what he

said and what he did. Granny wasn't as lucky as they all had thought she was going to be. Kenny slept until noon almost every day; when he did get up he went swimming with Andy, or they went fishing in *Josie's Coat* or just fooled around. Andy couldn't see that Kenny did anything for his grandmother. Once in awhile he was seen carrying rubbish out to the dump. Often when Andy was at Granny's house he heard her coaxing him to bring water from the well for drinking, or from the lake for washing, but most of the time she did it herself, limping along with her cane in one hand and the bucket in the other. Kenny usually found some excuse for not helping her, and if Andy were around he'd stand on Granny's blind side and wink at him broadly.

"Poor old soul," Mother said one day, "all that big lummox does is eat and sleep; he's eating her out of house and home. Why, he eats like a horse! I can't imagine how she makes her welfare money stretch."

Andy secretly thought Kenny's way of sneaking out of working was smart, although he had to admit even he felt a trifle ashamed when he saw the old lady struggling up the hill with her bucket of water.

"For heaven's sake, Andy," his mother called one day, "there goes Granny with a bucket of water. Run and carry it for her. Where d'you 'spose that lazy kid is?"

Andy knew very well where that lazy kid was; still sleeping, he hoped, because if he ever saw Andy carrying water up the hill for Granny he'd never have anything to do with him again. But nobody disobeyed Mary Thunder, to her face, anyway; so he ran after Granny and took her bucket. As he surmised, Kenny was still sleeping soundly when he slipped furtively into the house with it.

"Ssh! don't wake him up," he whispered to Granny and sneaked out of sight as quietly as he could.

One evening in July when the sun was beginning to slide down toward the Major's place, the two boys were sitting on the dock, as usual, Kenny restless and bored.

"How do you stand it here?" he demanded. "There ain't a damn thing to do!"

"Yeah," Andy agreed slowly, feeling a little ashamed, because until Kenny came he'd always thought Vermilion Reservation was a pretty good place, even if it was lonely. Of course, now he realized that was only because he was "a stupid reservation Indian," as Kenny had pointed out to him on numerous occasions.

"I know what let's do," Kenny said suddenly. "Let's take your boat and go over to town and get some beer."

Once more Andy didn't know what to do. "But Kenny!" he exclaimed, "we can't buy beer! You know that! We're minors; you have to be twenty-one before you can buy beer in Minnesota."

Kenny laughed. "What's the matter with you, kid?" he asked. "There're plenty of ways to get beer before you're twenty-one. I've been drinking beer for years. You've *tasted* it, haven't you?"

"Yeah, I've tasted it." Andy nodded reluctantly, because he had tasted it only once and hated it. "I know what," he suggested hopefully, "let's row over to town and get a Coke. I'll treat you to a Coke. I got paid a dollar today. You can even have a float if you want it, or a malted."

"Cokes! malteds!" Kenny sneered. "I'm sick to death of

baby stuff like that. It's all I've had since I came out to this place. I'm goin' to have a beer; you can have Coke if you want it, baby boy!"

Andy could feel the hot blood crawling up his face.

"OK, we'll go get beer, if you know how."

"Leave it to me," Kenny promised, getting up and jumping into *Josie's Coat*.

Andy got the oars, and they started out across the lake, heading for the shore where he had found *Josie*. The summer people were all here now, zooming across the lake in their sleek runabouts, trolling for walleyes around Whisky Island, swooping in graceful arcs on water skis. Andy kept thinking how wonderful it would be to have even a ten-horse motor for Josie. Rowing across Pike Bay to East Two River was an ordeal. Kenny never offered to take a turn rowing. Andy didn't know if he even knew how.

Andy rowed cautiously across the treacherous river channel, dotted with deadheads, and up the little waterway. They passed the new marina and tied *Josie* to a stake near the highway bridge. Kenny stopped at the first tavern they came to on the main street.

"Watch this, kid," he said.

He leaned nonchalantly against the wall, an unlit cigarette hanging on his lip and waited. Soon somebody came along, and started into the bar. He was a white man, probably in his twenties, and Kenny stepped over to him and said, in his most sophisticated manner,

"Hey, Bud, got a match?"

Andy, watching admiringly, thought Kenny could have passed for twenty-two, at least. The man lit the cigarette for him, and they began to talk. Finally Kenny took some money out of his pocket and said,

"Here's enough money for an extra beer for you if you'll bring us out a couple of cans in a bag."

So they got their beer and rowed back down the little river. The sun was gone now and the power boats were beginning to glide in from the lake and up to their moorings. *Josie* slipped along toward the lake, hugging the side of the narrow strip of water, rocking gently in the swells from the big boats. The boys had decided to stop at the beach beside the black tower and drink the beer, so Andy beached *Josie* on the strip of sand where he had found her, and they sat down on a log at the foot of the tower. Kenny opened his can and began to drink the beer in great gulps. Andy sipped at his, trying to figure out a way to get rid of it, but Kenny kept his eye on him, so he couldn't.

Finally, when he thought he would vomit if he took another drop, he threw the can far into the bushes and hoped it wasn't noticed in the dusk. Kenny finished his and smacked his lips.

"Gee, that was great, wasn't it?" he commented. "Sure lots better than a Coke. Now that you've learned to drink it, we'll have to come over here and get some often."

Andy could almost feel himself turning green. Fortunately Kenny didn't seem to expect an answer. He was feeling very good after his beer, so he suggested a race around the tower before they went home.

"It's getting pretty dark, and I haven't got a flashlight," Andy objected. "I think we'd better start back, or we'll get picked up by the water patrol."

"Aw come on, we need the exercise," Kenny urged. "It won't take a minute. I'll beat you."

He was off, and Andy followed him, stumbling over old bricks, stones and bushes in the twilight. They came to the door where men used to shovel ashes out of the huge incinerator when it was still used. The door was slightly ajar, and Kenny tugged it open.

"Ever been inside?" he asked, peering into the musty, dark interior.

"No!" Andy shuddered, jumping back.

"Well, here's your chance! Here you go!" Kenny yelled, giving Andy a shove through the door.

Andy landed on his hands and knees in the blackness. Before he could leap to his feet and dash out, Kenny had slammed the door shut and was dancing up and down, shouting with glee.

"Let me out!" Andy screamed, shoving at the door with all his strength.

It didn't give an inch; it was shut tight, and he began to beat on it with his hands and kick it with his feet, yelling at Kenny all the time to let him out. At last Kenny stopped laughing and began to pull at the door from the outside.

"Come on, come on," he shouted. "Quit being a baby. Push *hard*. You can open it if you try."

Andy was pushing as hard as he could, and the door wouldn't budge.

"I can't open it," he called, and his voice echoed hollowly in the depths of the old tower. "It must have some kind of a catch lock. What're we going to do, Kenny?"

For the first time Kenny's voice sounded scared and uncertain when he answered. "I dunno. Maybe you'll have to stay in there till morning and I can get some help. Nobody'll come way over here at night. Gee, it's spooky here."

"Oh no you don't!" Andy's voice rose to a scream again. "You get me out of here. You got me in."

Now Kenny's voice turned to a whine, "Well, what am I gonna do? Tell me that. D'you want me to walk all the way back to town for help? Who d'you know in town anyhow who'd come out to get you at night?"

Andy didn't know anybody, as long as Kenny put it that way, but his mind had begun working fast, once he realized that Kenny didn't know what to do.

"Get into the boat and row over to the Major's," he ordered, not caring that Kenny was three years older than he. "I know he'll come and get me out. Hurry up! It'll be pitch dark pretty soon."

"Not me!" Kenny yelled. "I couldn't row that old wreck that far. You'll be all right in there. Nothin' gonna hurt ya." He snickered and went on, "Nothin' can get in."

Andy began to remember the tales he had heard all his life about the tower—the talk about its being haunted, and about ghosts, evil spirits, rats and snakes inside of it. He heard something rustle in the dark and broke out in a cold sweat.

"You go for the Major right now, or I'll get even with you, Kenny," Andy shrieked. "I'm not telling you what it will be, but I'll get you for this."

The sound of Kenny's callous snicker still echoed in his ears, and he was boiling mad.

"Oh, all right. I'll go, but I expect to drown," Kenny said after a long minute of silence.

Suddenly Andy realized, in the midst of his own fear, that Kenny was really afraid to go on the water at night, and he wondered once more if Kenny even knew how to row.

"You won't drown if you watch out for deadheads and keep out of the way of boats in the bay," he assured him. "Hurry up!"

Kenny didn't say anymore, but in a minute Andy heard the bottom of the boat scraping on the gravel, then the oars squeaking in the locks, and knew Kenny was on his way. He heaved a sigh of relief and tried to figure out how long it would take to get there and back. Coming back wouldn't take long because the Major would come in his power boat. Maybe an hour and they'd be there.

How long would an hour seem when he was shut up in the tower all alone? It would seem an eternity if he didn't do something, but he didn't dare move away from the door in the blackness. There could easily be things around he could trip on. He wondered what else might be in the tower. All sorts of creatures could have slipped in through that crack in the door. Most of them harmless, but maybe not all.

Time dragged on and he thought he *must* sit down, he was so tired; but then there were rustling sounds, maybe his feet scuffling in the ancient ashes, and maybe not. The top of the tower was open to the sky with only a cover of rusty screen over it. When he first looked up, the sky was still a deep blue with wisps of rosy sunset clouds floating across the opening. Now all was dark with only a few stars like tiny pinpricks of light through black paper.

He had no way of knowing how long it had been since Kenny started out across the end of Pike Bay to the Major's house. It might have been an hour; it might have been two or three. Where was Kenny now? Andy knew he couldn't be much good with the oars, and *Josie's Coat* was tricky to maneuver. She had a habit of going crooked like a dog running with a crooked hind leg; you had to pull a little harder on the right oar all the time or she would land you where you didn't want to go. Had Kenny rowed into a deadhead in the channels, or let *Josie* get him mired down in the weed bed along the shore, or might he have turned too sharply around the point of land that jutted out into the bay where he must turn west? Andy knew there were rocks just under the surface of the water there, but he doubted that Kenny would remember. He could rip the bottom right out of the old boat if he ran onto them in the darkness.

The more Andy thought about Kenny rowing in the dark without even the moon to light the way, the surer he was that there would be trouble. He might sink *Josie's Coat,* and then what? If Kenny drowned, nobody would know where Andy was or what had happened to him. By the time he heard the noise of a motor coming closer in the night, he had almost accepted the idea that he might even die all alone in the gloom of the tower. But that surely was a motor that he heard, and it must be the Major coming for him. His shouts echoed and reechoed in the vast emptiness around him.

The sound of the motor grew louder and then began to diminish; great waves of disappointment washed over him. It was just another power boat, late in returning to its mooring up little East Two River. Of course, the people in the boat couldn't hear his shouts above the noise of the motor as they went by. He shuffled back to the door, sliding his hands along the cold, clammy iron wall; it was inky black now, and even with his eyes accustomed to it, he couldn't see anything. Just then something ran across his foot, and that did it!

He didn't scream, there was nobody to hear a scream. He simply froze against the side of the tower, pressing his body against it. He had no idea how long he huddled there, rigid as the walls of the towers themselves. The rustling sounds and little animal squeaks continued, things that wouldn't have bothered him at all in the daylight. Once in awhile a loon cried over the lake, the loneliest sound on earth. He shut off his mind for the time being, and all he was aware of during those endless minutes or hours, was the muted sound of a motor far off on the lake, or the muffled roar of a giant trailer truck plunging through the night up on the highway.

The motor on the lake never came close, and he thought vaguely that it was probably the water patrol cruising around looking for boats without lights. He almost hoped one of them would pick Kenny up. The sound would fade away across the water, however, and he would return to his dazed waiting.

It didn't seem as though he could possibly have fallen asleep on his feet in the cold, frightful darkness of the tower, but he didn't hear the motor coming. He heard nothing until the Major was calling to him from the other side of the door, and he could hear him prying at it with tools and giving Kenny instructions.

"Hang on, Andy," the voice was saying. "We'll have you out of there in a minute!"

He broke the rusty old lock and pulled the door open. The cool, sweet lake air poured over Andy, and he stumbled out to ride home in the Major's big boat.

eight

Andy's mother was furious at both boys. She had been frantic when darkness came and they weren't home; then when they finally appeared and she smelled beer on their breath she was madder yet. She read the riot act to Kenny for giving Andy beer and shutting him up in the tower; then sent him packing up the hill to his grandmother and continued her lecture to Andy alone.

"You have no business drinking beer," she stormed. "You're too young, and besides, I don't want you drinking beer."

"I know," Andy agreed meekly. "You don't have to worry. I'll never touch it again. It makes me sick."

It was surprising, though, how quickly he got over that and began sneaking over to town every time he got a chance to have a can of beer with Kenny. His mother didn't talk about it after that first night, but she knew what was going on, all right. Sometimes he would catch her looking at him with a strange expression in her black eyes—half sad, half angry. She didn't need to put her feelings into words. She ignored Kenny completely, and he stayed out of her way as much as possible.

Andy was lost without Johnny that summer. He hadn't realized how much he had depended upon him as a person to talk to, in the woods. It would have been good to talk to him now, for he did have problems, even though he wouldn't admit it to his mother or scarcely to himself. Often he had a day full of the "wrong feeling" that had come over him early in the summer. Kenny was no good to him then because he was such an aimless drifter himself. Andy never tried to talk to him about the uneasy feeling that kept plaguing him, but when it got really bad he'd just say,

"Let's go over to town, Kenny," and away they'd go in *Josie's Coat.*

He couldn't say that the trips to town did much for him, except to take his mind off his troubles for a little while. The final result was even worse, however, because it left him with miserable guilt feelings. Sometimes he even wished his mother would blow up at him again, instead of just looking at him with that sad-angry look.

When he and Kenny bought beer, they usually took it back to the tower and sat beside it in the dusk and talked. Neither one of them ever went near the door again, and they never talked about that night! They had other things to discuss. Kenny had another year of high school to do, and he wasn't happy about it. His mother was writing to him all the time now, insisting that he come home and get a job for the rest of the summer so he could buy school clothes.

"Gosh Andy, you're lucky, not having to go to school!" he

would say frequently. "Your ma don't care if you go or not, does she?"

A peculiar feeling would flash over Andy when Kenny said things like that. He would feel strangely defensive and protective toward his mother, even though he refused to face the thought of going back to school. Kenny didn't understand; he didn't know how terribly she cared because Andy wasn't going to school. Finally, he couldn't stand it any longer, so he let loose one night, summoning the courage to say what he really felt.

"She does too care," he shouted, getting up and pacing back and forth in the long grass. "She cares, all right, but she doesn't yell at me about it all the time the way your old lady does! You lay off my mother! I don't want to hear you say anything against her anymore. You just shut up!"

Kenny sat up with a puzzled, hurt frown on his face. "I wasn't saying anything against her," he protested. "I told you, I think you're lucky."

When Andy thought it over afterward, he was surprised that Kenny hadn't taken a good swing at him. He didn't honestly know why he had been so rough with him.

It was the next day that Johnny came to Lake Vermilion at last. Without any warning he came walking around the corner of the house. Andy was swimming off the dock and came rushing up to grab his hand. His mother was in the house patching blue jeans. The sun shining through the window lay on the blue-black braids coiled around her head, and burnished her copper-gold skin. Andy tugged impatiently at his hand, and Johnny, never taking his eyes from the picture she made there in the sunshine, whispered,

"Hold your horses, *gwe-we-zance,* it'll be your turn in a minute."

Mary Thunder heard him and stood up. She dropped her sewing on her chair and took a step toward Johnny, now standing in the doorway. Andy wondered what they would do, these two people who had been half in love, long ago. He watched in fascination as though he were at a movie. His mother moved slowly toward Johnny and held out both her hands; he took them gently in his big ones, but still not a word had been spoken. They just stood silently in the summer sun and looked at each other. Andy could only wonder what thoughts were passing between them. Then Johnny said softly, in his deep voice,

"Mary Thunder, prettiest *equay-zance* I ever saw!"

Andy's mother pulled her hands away and laughed in the special way she had when she was happy. The spell was broken, and all of them began to talk at once. Johnny had driven over from Nett Lake in his old car that morning because he had some business in town, and of course he wanted to see Andy. They persuaded him to stay a day or two and invited him to stay with them, but he refused because he said it would be too crowded; he would stay with his cousin. He went over to see her while Mother mixed fresh bannock dough and made a pot of coffee. Ellen and Rosemary came in from the woods with a pail of wild blackberries for lunch. When Johnny came back, Mary Thunder was frying the bannocks, and the heavenly fragrance drifted out into the warm summer day.

They spent all of the afternoon catching up on happenings since they had been apart. Johnny admired *Josie's Coat,* laughed at the name and thought it was great that Andy had her to play around with. He had retired from his job in the woods because an old back injury had flared up this summer. He would get some partial disability insurance because of it, but he was looking for some kind of light work that wouldn't require any heavy lifting. In the meantime he was thinking seriously of moving to Vermilion Reservation to live with his cousin.

"She's getting old, and you probably know she can't see so good now," he explained to them. "It's tough on her, living alone, 'specially in the winter. She's been at me to come over here to live, and I think mebbe I will."

He smiled at them, and they all smiled back because they couldn't think of anything better than to have Johnny for a neighbor! While Andy was thinking how wonderful it would be, he was dragged rudely back to his own problems by Johnny's next remark:

"When do you start back to school?" he asked abruptly.

Andy was so taken aback, he was speechless for a moment. Then he said rather sharply, looking out of the corners of his eyes at his mother,

"Why Johnny, you know I'm not going back to school. We talked about that the first time we met, and I haven't changed my mind at all."

His mother sat silent and expressionless, looking out over the lake, and Johnny's face took on the grim, somber look that Andy had seen it wear a few times before. He didn't say anything for a few minutes, and then he shook his head and said,

"I hoped you'd changed your mind. What do you do all day?"

Andy was on the defensive instantly.

"Well," he explained, "there aren't very many jobs this summer for boys, and you know I'm not sixteen yet. I'm doing odd jobs now, cutting grass 'n' stuff. Next year when I'm sixteen, I'll be getting a good job."

"Oh? Like what?" Johnny pressured him.

"Well, I don't know for sure yet, but probably I'll be working in a store or maybe even a factory, or something," he petered out lamely.

Johnny gave him a long, penetrating look, and then he said to Andy's mother,

"Mary, what do you think about this boy and school? Your other kids finished high school, didn't they?"

"Oh yes," she answered, "all the older ones finished, and some of them have even finished college. Two of the boys will be in college this fall. I've just got Andy, Harry and the girls to go."

Both of them were looking at Andy, and he could feel the red flooding his face.

"Andy, what makes you think you're so much smarter than the rest of your family that you don't have to go to school?" Johnny asked him. It sounded funny, but Andy didn't laugh because he knew it wasn't meant to be funny. It was deadly serious. He was really flustered now; in the past he had been able to wriggle out of the discussion somehow and get the subject changed, but he was afraid this was going to be the showdown, and he wasn't sure that he could take those two on single-handed and win the bout.

"I don't think I'm any better than anybody," he protested miserably. "It was just that I had such a bad time in school. Everybody thought I was dumb—" He let the sentence trail off into the sunny afternoon air.

"And the rabbit head bounced down the steps," Johnny took up his story as if from memory, "and Andy was so weak he let the bouncing rabbit head bounce him right out of school for the rest of his life!"

Andy was crushed. Johnny had never spoken so harshly to him before, and he didn't know how to cope with it. His mother saw his predicament and saved him temporarily by changing the subject, but Andy knew he hadn't heard the last of school. He almost wished Johnny had stayed back at Nett Lake where he belonged and minded his own business. But then, as he went down to the dock and sat there alone, he reluctantly came to the conclusion that after all this *was* Johnny's business, almost as much as it was Mother's and his. When he remembered what Johnny had done for him when he found him bleeding and penniless in Ely, he could hardly ask Johnny to mind his own business!

nine

Kenny came along with a friend from the city as Andy was sitting on the dock. Jeff was a white boy who lived near Kenny and had come up to visit for a few days. They went over to see the tent he had pitched in Granny Kingfisher's yard, and before Andy left, they had made plans for the evening. They would ride into town after supper in Jeff's car, and have a drink of something.

"Jeff's twenty-one and he's got a good job, so the sky's the limit tonight." Kenny winked at Andy.

It was too bad to leave Johnny the first night he was there, but Andy had learned that you didn't refuse the fellows when they asked you out for a drink, or you didn't get asked again. And he was still a little mad at Johnny, anyhow.

Jeff's car was a convertible. They put the top down and rode into town like millionaires. Instead of stopping at the bar right away, they picked up some beer at a supermarket and went down the highway to Ely, flying along, covering in less than thirty minutes the miles it had taken Andy so long to walk. Then they decided to drive out to Angleworm Lake so the guys could see where he had worked all winter. The sun was setting when they turned off Echo Trail onto the narrow, hilly road that led down to camp. The buildings were all boarded up and deserted. They got out and walked down to the lake. Andy told them about his trouble with Bad Bill and how he was nearly choked to death by him the day Bill left camp. Just telling about it gave him goosepimples all over again. It was worth it though, because they were quite impressed.

An hour later they drove back down the trail, headed for town and the bar. After the beers they had had on the way, Andy felt he didn't need anything more. But Kenny and Jeff were anticipating what Jeff called his "surprise," so Andy decided not to be a wet blanket. Jeff parked near the tavern and went in to get it. It was a surprise, all right. He came out with a bottle of brandy. Even Kenny's eyes popped at that.

"Where can we go to drink it?" Jeff asked. "I don't want to get busted because you guys are minors."

Andy couldn't think where they could go that late at night and not have somebody wonder what was going on.

"Aw, don't be such fraidycats, you two guys. It's so dark now, we can sit right here in the car and take turns drinking out of the bottle and nobody'll even notice," scoffed Kenny. "I dare you!"

Andy didn't like the idea much, but they sat there, right smack in front of the tavern on the main street, drinking brandy out of the bottle and getting louder and rowdier by the minute. Andy noticed that the others' voices were rising and their laughs were more and more boisterous, but he couldn't hear himself being the same way. He was afraid the only policeman in town would come along and pick them up, but nobody on the street seemed to pay any attention to them.

Suddenly the door of the tavern swung open violently and a short, rotund man plummeted out onto the sidewalk beside the car. He was roaring drunk and obviously had been kicked out of the bar. Andy wasn't so far gone that he couldn't recognize that voice. He would have known it anywhere in the world, under any circumstances.

He was sitting on the outside toward the curb and he edged closer to Kenny in the middle and whispered into his ear,

"My God! That's Bad Bill. Be quiet! If he sees me I'm a goner."

Kenny thought Andy's remark was hilariously funny. He shouted with laughter and yelled drunkenly at Jeff,

"Did you hear that, Jeff? Guess who that is. It's Andy's pal, Bad Bill, the guy he told us about. Fancy meeting him here!"

Addled as he was, Andy knew that the danger was real and immediate. He clapped his hand over Kenny's mouth and huddled down in the seat as far as he could.

"Start the car, Jeff," he implored. "Let's get out of here, quick!"

But Jeff's reflexes were in no condition to do anything quick. While he fumbled with the ignition key, Bad Bill had time to see who was in the car by the light over the tavern door. Drunk or sober, he was quick as a cat, and he knew Andy. Instantly he swung toward him, dragged him from the seat and over the side of the car. He lost contact for a split second, and if Andy had been himself he would have taken advantage of the chance to run. His legs were longer than Bill's and far more agile; he could outrun him, and would have had no guilty pangs about running away from a fight. Nobody with a grain of sense would have felt cowardly running from Bad Bill in a fighting mood. Andy could have run, but he didn't because suddenly all that brandy inside of him turned him into a fighting tiger. He leaped at Bill with all his strength and speed and for a moment the man reeled back, taken by surprise, but then he let out a roar like an enraged jungle animal and attacked. He had Andy on the sidewalk in a second, and they rolled and kicked, with him bellowing all the time.

"Nobody rat on Bad Bill and get away with it! I'll kill you this time!"

At first Andy thought he was doing pretty well, and a wave of pride flooded over him when he realized he was able to stay on top part of the time and hold his own.

"He's old," Andy thought to himself, "and awfully drunk. I'll wear him down; I'll beat him! I'm young and strong."

He was young and he was strong, but it was soon obvious even to him that he was no match for the old master of dirty fighting, clawing, scratching and kicking.

In a little while quite a sizable crowd had gathered from somewhere to watch, late as it was. Gradually Andy's strength began to wane, and he was panting desperately, sucking in every breath, gasping to stay conscious. He was on the bottom all the time now, feeling as though Bad Bill's heavy body were crushing the life out of him.

"Where's Officer Mulhagen?" somebody in the crowd shouted.

"Gone fishin'," somebody answered. "He ain't back yet."

Andy, half gone, thought wildly about the boys. Had they driven away and just left him there to die all alone? He hadn't enough breath left to call out to them. One of his eyes was closed, and the lid was bleeding. He could feel the blood trickling into it. The other eye was still open, but he couldn't see much out of it because his face was under Bad Bill's knee and he had the feeling his head was being ground into the concrete sidewalk.

He was very near the end of his rope. His mind was wandering from the liquor and from the ghastly, insane beating he had absorbed, but Andy could still think clearly enough to know that Bad Bill meant what he said, he intended to kill him, and this time he wouldn't miss. Andy wondered why nobody came to help him. Were those people just going to stand there? Would they let him be killed? Not even try to help him? Wouldn't even one of them risk anything to help an Indian?

He felt the end approaching. Bad Bill with a final mighty heave and a wild yell lifted him above his head and hurled him down against the rough stucco of the tavern wall, and Andy believed he had died. A cold black cloud descended upon him, and he knew nothing more. Actually he couldn't have been out very long. When he finally struggled back to life, pushing away the suffocating black fog, he heard men shouting and someone saying,

"I seen this here guy, Bad Bill, hangin' around here lately. He's a terror!"

69

Then he heard racing feet coming down the sidewalk toward him and a man's angry voice saying,

"You contemptible bully, attacking a kid! You get out of town fast and stay out. If you so much as show your face here again, you'll get what's coming to you! *Now go!*"

Andy heard a murmur of approval from the crowd, and then the same man speaking again, still with his voice sounding scornful and angry,

"And what was the matter with all you people? Couldn't even one of you help this boy? You're just as contemptible as that bully, every one of you! Maybe someone will be brave enough to go for the doctor. Can't you see this youngster's hurt *bad?*"

Andy blacked out again after that. For awhile his consciousness came and went in waves of pain. During one of his moments of comparative alertness he felt someone bending over him, and heard the same voice, speaking gently this time, to him.

"Can you hear me, boy?"

Andy could hear him, but he couldn't see him. He kept blinking his good eye and trying to see who it was. Finally a face swam into his line of vision for a minute, and he could see that it was a white man, one he didn't know, kneeling beside him. Very carefully he lifted Andy's head onto his lap and asked,

"What's your name; do you live here in town? Can you tell me that?"

Andy tried to speak, but couldn't make the sounds come. A man standing by said,

"No, he don't live in town. I've seen him around here be-

70

fore, though. He's from the reservation over on the lake."

Someone else stepped up close and stared down at him.

"Oh sure, I know now. He's one of Mary Thunder's kids. There's a whole raft of 'em. Their pa run off and left her with 'em."

The man holding Andy's head said quietly,

"I'm glad we know who he is. Maybe someone ought to go for his mother. This youngster's in pretty bad shape."

Andy heard a car drive up and stop just as he finished speaking, and footsteps running toward them.

"What happened? Let me through," he heard a familiar voice demanding.

A dark form leaned close to him, and the voice spoke again,

"Andy! *Gwe-we-zance!* Speak to me. It's Johnny."

Hearing his voice and glimpsing his face in the dim light brought Andy back to full consciousness. He struggled to sit up, but it hurt so much that he sank back, this time into Johnny's arms. The white man had let Johnny take his place, but he was still kneeling nearby.

"I don't think he should sit up," he said. "His cuts are still bleeding a good deal. Did anyone find Doc?"

"Coming," someone said.

The doctor was there. He pushed back the crowd and knelt beside Andy, looking him over carefully, feeling his injuries lightly.

"Well," he said at last, standing up and looking around at the people who still watched, "I don't think we have any broken bones, but it's a miracle he didn't fracture his skull, the way he got manhandled. We'll take him over to my

71

place, and I'll sew him up. If he's still groggy in the morning, we'll have some x-rays at the hospital."

"Do you know him, Doc?" someone asked.

"Sure do know him," the doctor replied. "Fact is, I delivered him. Mary Thunder had kind of a tough time with this one, so we took her into the hospital. Yep, I remember Andy real well."

He gave Andy a pat on the shoulder and said to Johnny,

"Let's put him in my car."

Together they lifted him and laid him on the back seat of Doc's car, and Johnny held his head in his lap again. The white man got into the front seat beside Doc, and they drove the few blocks to his house. His wife, who was a nurse, was waiting in the small office for him to come home. When he was called out at night on an injury case, she always knew she might be needed. So in a few minutes Andy was lying on the table, the doctor was scrubbing his hands and putting on rubber gloves, and his wife was gently washing the cuts with soap and water. It hurt so bad that he had to bite his tongue to keep from crying out. Then she put something on them to deaden the pain a little, and the doctor went about the business of stitching them up.

The three men talked while it was going on, and dazed though Andy was, he heard enough of the conversation to piece together some of it. Johnny told the white man and Doc who he was, and the other man shook hands with him and introduced himself as Bob Underhill, a teacher at the high school in town.

"It sure was lucky you happened to come along just when you did, Mr. Hawk," he said. "I was just about to send somebody for Andy's mother."

"I didn't just happen along," Johnny replied grimly. "The good-for-nothings Andy was with took off while he was fighting. They come to the lake and said Andy was hurt bad and I better come." He paused a moment and then went on, and Andy could tell by the sound of his voice that he was very angry. "Then they ran away, back to the city, I guess. A good thing for them. I'll clean up on them if I ever see them again. The yellow-livered cowards!"

"Yes, it was a good thing for them that they went back to the city," Bob Underhill agreed. "I'm sure Officer Mulhagen would have tossed them into jail when he got back from his fishing trip. Those guys could be prosecuted for contributing to the delinquency of a minor if the Thunders wanted to bring suit."

"No!" Andy exclaimed explosively.

Johnny looked down at him in silence for a moment or two and then said to the white teacher,

"No, Andy is right. The family has no money for a trial. Besides, Indians have a hard time at court against the white man."

"I suppose you're right, more's the pity," Bob Underhill answered.

The doctor was through, finally, and stood back to admire his handiwork.

"You'll have some scars for awhile, Andy," he said, "but you're young and the cuts will heal fast, and they won't show much by the time you grow up. The one in your forehead is the worst, and your hair will cover that when it grows back. It took twenty stitches to close you up."

Then he turned to the men and said,

"I want to keep him in town tonight so I can see him in

the morning. If he's still not tiptop, I'll want to x-ray, but I think he's going to be all right. We'd keep him here, but our kids are both home for the summer so we haven't room. Any suggestions? Do the Thunders have any friends in town?"

"Sure," Bob spoke up immediately. "We'll take him to my house. There's plenty of room there; only Ann, the baby and me."

Johnny walked back downtown for his car and Andy was put into it and taken a few blocks farther on and unloaded at the Underhills' house. Bob's wife, Ann, greeted them warmly, and Andy watched her hustling around making up the studio couch in Bob's study with smooth white sheets, and he heard the soft little mother-hen sounds she made when she looked at his bandages and bruises. Bob told her very briefly about Andy's fight and how he had just been returning from a late walk in time to help a little. Ann and the baby had been asleep when he slipped out, after a long evening of work.

Johnny helped Bob put Andy to bed, and then he went off in his old car to tell Andy's mother what had happened. Andy could hear it chugging down the street and finally the noise dying away.

Ann gave him one of the sleeping pills Doc had sent home with Bob, and in a little while he was asleep.

ten

The baby's crying awoke Andy in the morning. The small, book-filled room was flooded with sunshine; he lay there flexing his muscles and stretching experimentally to see if he was all in one piece. He seemed to be, but he was stiff and sore and his cuts hurt. The terrible headache of the night before had given way to a hangover from the brandy, but even with that he felt much better. At least he was firmly anchored to the world again. He didn't feel as though he were about to float off into space.

Ann came to the door and peeked in at him. She had the baby boy under one arm and Andy's clothes under the other.

"Good morning," she said coming over to him. "How's the head, Andy? My, but you do look better this morning!"

"I feel better, too," Andy said.

He sat up cautiously in Bob's pajamas, getting a good look at Ann for the first time. One eye was still swollen shut, but this morning he could focus the other. Ann and the baby were both smiling at him, but he couldn't smile back because one of his twenty stitches was close to the corner of his mouth.

"D'you feel like getting dressed and having some breakfast?" she wanted to know. "Your clothes were the dirtiest, bloodiest mess I've ever seen, but I soaked them in cold water and let them perk in the washer for a long time, so I think they turned out quite well. How about some milk toast? It should be best for that sore mouth."

She departed with Bobby hanging over her shoulder, and Andy stood up, wobbly and hurting, but able to walk. Bob Underhill came in while Andy dressed to give him a hand. They were to go to the doctor after breakfast and then, if everything was OK, Andy would go home. Ann had set the table in the kitchen, and they all sat down to eat.

Andy supposed it was a modest house, but it looked wonderful to him; he had never been in one so pretty. There were yellow curtains at the windows and a yellow cloth on the table with a glass bowl of daisies in the middle. Ann handed him warm milk toast in a blue pottery bowl. She had broken the toast into little bite-size pieces and put a straw in his glass of orange juice so he could drink it easily. He sat in the sun and ate his breakfast very slowly and listened to the others talk because it hurt when he tried.

After breakfast he and Bob went to see Doc. He looked Andy over carefully again and said,

"Well, young one, I guess you can go home, and we won't need x-rays. Do you know what a close call you had? That madman came awful close to killing you!"

"That's what he was aiming to do," Andy mumbled out of the good corner of his mouth.

Then he told as briefly as he could about Bad Bill in the lumber camp. After that Doc wanted to know why he hadn't been in school last year, so he had to explain that, and before he got through Doc wanted to know what brought them to the tavern at midnight. Andy decided that Doc was the snoopiest man he had ever known!

"Now one more thing before I let you go," he said, looking sternly at Andy. "Last night there was liquor on your breath, and it wasn't beer that I smelled; that would have been bad enough at fifteen, but it was hard liquor. You're much too young for that, and besides, Mary Thunder deserves better from you. She's had a hard time bringing you kids up alone. Now go home and let her see that you're all right and let's have no more night life for a long time! Come back in a week, and we'll see about those stitches. In the meantime you don't need to stay in bed, but keep quiet for a few days."

A little later as Bob Underhill and Andy turned off the main road and drove through the woods that led to the village, Bob asked if this land belonged to the reservation. Andy explained that it had been theirs originally, but they had leased a good deal of it, including the best lakeshore frontage, to white people for summer places. Bob shook his head and frowned as though that disturbed him, but he said nothing more until they drove down the hill onto the smooth meadowland where the village lay.

Mother and Johnny were sitting outdoors, waiting. Ellen and Rosemary ran up from the dock. Andy thought Mr. Underhill would just leave and go right home, but he parked the car in back of the house and got out. He shook hands with Johnny and Andy's mother and sat down at her invitation. Because Andy knew her so well, he understood without a word being spoken that she was deeply concerned about him, upset because he had let such a calamity happen, and worried about his future, but she didn't say so. She would talk to him about it some other time, but not now, in the presence of a stranger, and a white stranger at that.

Her face was quite impassive as her glance slid over his swollen eye and his cuts and bruises. He wondered if Mr. Underhill thought she didn't care. He wished his mother would say something, anything, to show that she did care.

The silence continued, and just as it began to seem unbearable, his mother came over to him and laid her hand gently against his forehead, as she used to do when he was little and sick. She never had a thermometer in the house.

"No fever," she said with satisfaction, and then turning in sudden fury to the men, she cried,

"That man must have been a mad beast!"

That was all she needed to say. Mr. Underhill nodded, and Johnny said,

"He was a mad beast, Mary. Now let's forget this and talk about Andy and what to do about him."

They talked almost as if he, Andy, were not there, the three adults drawn together in a close little knot, pausing only now and then to cast a speculative glance at him. They didn't seem much concerned about his injuries. Instead they were discussing his return to school in the fall. When Andy realized the turn the conversation was taking he stood up shakily and tried to assert himself in spite of his sore, cut mouth.

"Now just a minute," he mumbled, shaking his finger to get their attention.

Johnny waved him back down on the grass, and Andy thought he was actually nasty the way he said,

"We've had enough of your 'just a minutes' Andy. Now you just wait a minute yourself. You listen to us for a change. You haven't done so well for yourself lately."

So Andy subsided and listened, because he had to admit to himself that Johnny was right; he'd done a pretty lousy job this summer. They went on talking and when the discussion ended, it had been decided that Andy would go back to school in the fall. Nobody seemed to notice his efforts to protest, until at last Bob Underhill spoke.

"Sorry, Andy," he said. "We certainly should have included you in the discussion. We just didn't think."

"No," Andy's mother said very frankly, "I, at least, didn't forget you, Andrew. It just hasn't been possible to discuss this subject reasonably with you all summer. You know that! You wouldn't even talk about it with me."

"Well, I'll talk about it now," Andy said, forgetting all about how his mouth hurt. "I can't imagine why all of you people think it's such a great idea to push me back into high school. I don't need to go to high school to be a success."

"Your older brothers and sisters all graduated from high school," his mother interrupted.

"Well," Andy retorted hotly, "that doesn't mean that I have to go to high school just because they did. They didn't go to our high school. Don't you know that Indians *never* graduate from our high school? Billy went to Virginia, Helen went to Duluth, Edward went to Eveleth, and you sent the other girls out to South Dakota to that church boarding school, but none of them ever went to ours. Indian kids who go to our high school always flunk out."

Bob Underhill had been sitting on the grass beside Andy, listening carefully to the argument.

"Andy," he said, "aren't you smart enough to know that if you don't go to school this fall and stay until you're sixteen, the truant officer will be after you? This isn't a lumber camp in the deep woods."

Andy nodded reluctantly and Bob went on, "Now, we know all about the rabbit head and the trouble you had in school with math and English, and the long johns and phys. ed., but not one of them was big enough nor important enough to keep you from getting an education. I'm quite sure, without any tests, that you're a bright boy, you can learn, and you can graduate."

He shifted his position and cleared his throat, "I'll be perfectly honest with you and tell you that your biggest problem is probably going to be the other kids, and that's because they haven't learned yet how to get along with people of a different race. It's mostly our fault and we're working at it, but we've still got a ways to go. If you go back, understanding that, and you've got the guts to stick, you'll make it."

eleven

Andy went back to school in September. Bob Underhill tutored him in math, his weakest subject, every day all the rest of the summer, and Ann helped him with English, which she had taught before the baby came. Andy mowed their lawn and weeded the garden and watched Bobby several afternoons a week to pay for it. He was so busy that he didn't have time to worry about September. When it actually came and he took the school bus to town and walked up those long steps again, it really wasn't so bad.

He went with the understanding that he could quit when his sixteenth birthday came if he simply couldn't stand it. His mother and Johnny had agreed to that. But by the time his birthday came, things were going rather well. He was actually proud of his math marks, and he went out for swimming in the winter and track in the spring. When he won the hundred-yard dash at a county track meet in May, there was no more talk of his dropping out of school, though he did still want a job, at least for the summer.

All winter Andy kept dropping in at the boatyard to talk about a summer job. Johnny thought they'd get sick to death of him, but evidently they didn't, because he got a pretty good job there when school was out. Nothing serious happened with the white kids, at least nothing that he couldn't handle. Maybe his newfound talents in swimming and track helped some; anyhow, by the end of the year they didn't seem to think of Andy as just a dumb Indian kid anymore. He couldn't say that he was exactly chummy with any of them, but they were reasonably polite. Since he was doing well in his classes, the teachers were accepting him better, too.

The next year there were a few more Indians in the school, and best of all there was a new Indian boy named Pete. He had moved with his family from Nett Lake over to the Vermilion Reservation. The two boys liked each other immediately. Pete was a senior, but even so they often studied together. Pete kept Andy going sometimes when he might otherwise have bogged down. Though he was doing quite well, even making the honor roll the last semester that year, he was still obsessed with the fear that he might not graduate because "no Indian ever graduates from our high school." It helped a little when Pete graduated with honors that spring, but Andy was still uneasy about himself.

Pete tried to talk him out of it. "You've got to get rid of that hang-up, Andy," he said several times, "or come graduation night you'll walk up to get your diploma and instead of saying, 'Thank you, sir,' you'll absentmindedly say, 'Sorry, but there must be some mistake. No Indian ever graduates from our high school.' "

82

They both laughed, but it did Andy good to have Pete tease him, and eventually he didn't brood so much. As his second year in high school passed, it became apparent that he was going to graduate, almost in spite of himself. So many people were pushing him along that he could scarcely help it. Mother and Johnny encouraged him at home. After Johnny moved over to the village to live, he spent a lot of time at their house. He would sit there talking to Andy about school while he kept his eyes on Mary Thunder as she washed dishes or sewed. He would say, tamping fresh tobacco down into his pipe,

"You see, Andy, if I had gone to school I could help you with that math problem. You have to go to school so you can help your children with theirs."

Then he would laugh uproariously. Andy didn't think it was funny at all. He thought math was an invention of the devil, in spite of Bob Underhill's tutoring. For the Underhills had stayed right with him and did all they could for him. For example, Bob always seemed to know when a big math test was coming up, even though Andy wasn't in his class. And, although she wasn't teaching, Ann seemed to have heard when he had a quiz in English or an important theme due. So there was always extra help then.

One other thing that happened had a great deal to do with keeping Andy in school. He was supposed to be getting a "free education," but he soon learned that there were a lot of things that weren't free. Very soon after school started the first year, he discovered there was a substantial fee for a stu-dent-affairs ticket, which included athletic events, dances, school plays and practically every social event of any kind.

Mr. Underhill called Andy into his room after school one day and asked if he were going to the football game that evening. Of course Andy wasn't because he didn't have a student-affairs ticket. He hadn't had the money to pay for one. Everyone had been told that if he couldn't afford to buy one, he should tell his homeroom teacher about it and "arrangements" would be made. But who would do that?

He hated to tell Bob why he didn't have a ticket, but Bob didn't wait for an answer,

"I'm glad you don't have a ticket yet because I have an extra one," he said, pulling one out of his pocket." I got to thinking that if you hadn't bought yours, you could use this one. It's too bad to have it go to waste, and if you hang onto it, you'll be able to get into all the social things all year, free."

"Thanks," Andy said stiffly, "but I don't accept charity."

Some advice Johnny had given him once while they were in the woods flashed into his mind. He had been paying an installment on his debt when Johnny said suddenly,

"*Always be proud,* Andy, whether you've got anything to be proud about or not!"

"This isn't charity, Andy," Bob assured him. "A man I know gave me some money for what I like to call my 'discretionary fund.' It's a fund I can use to buy small things for boys who can use them. It's a kind of memorial for a son this man used to have."

Andy looked at him silently for awhile and then decided that he was telling the truth.

"OK," he said, "just as long as you aren't making up this man and it isn't *your* money."

Bob threw back his head and laughed, and then he said,

"Why Andy, you know I don't have any extra money to throw around. I work on the road most of summer vacations to be able to support my family. I'd like nothing better than to buy you a student-affairs ticket myself, but all we can do for you is give you a little free tutoring and ask you to dinner once in awhile. Now come on, don't be stuffy, eh? Make this man happy by using his money. I'm not making him up; I'd tell you who he is, but he insists upon remaining anonymous. He's a very real man."

Andy put the ticket in his pocket, and that was the first of many times that Bob thought of special things he needed and couldn't have unless the wonderful fund could afford them. Andy never asked him for even the smallest amount. It seemed to him if he did it would vanish like the magic pot of gold in the old fairy tales. Yet the money always seemed to be there just when he needed it.

twelve

"If he went to Bemidji we could see him more often," Andy's mother said with a wistful tone in her voice.

"Oh Mom!" his oldest brother objected, "if he goes to Bemidji, he'll be just another reservation Indian—it's too near home."

"There's UMD, the University of Minnesota branch at Duluth," Ann suggested. "It's a good school, and not too far away."

"I've got to go to a college where they'll take me," Andy said practically, reverting back to the days when he didn't have much confidence in his own ability.

"Which is the cheapest?" Johnny wanted to know. "Andy can't afford an expensive school."

It was the first week of Andy's senior year, and they were all sitting out in front of the house on the grass discussing his college plans. It reminded Andy of the day when almost the same people had gathered in the same place to decide whether or not he should go to high school. But now the subject was college, and not whether he would go, but where. Now and then he thought he'd like to make his own decision, but he knew he couldn't because money was such a big part of deciding. And he was going to need help with money wherever he went.

Bob had been lounging comfortably on the grass, staring off across the lake at the trees on the other side. Now he sat up straight.

"I don't want Andy to decide where he's going to college on the basis of any of these things," he began. "You've got a good scholarship record, Andy, in spite of your slow start. Many schools would be glad to have you. It would be nice to have you near home, of course, but I don't think we should be selfish about that, so let's forget it and think of Johnny's remark about money."

He smiled at Andy and said, "I hope you haven't got your heart set on the Ivy League, Andy, because I doubt if we can manage that, but we ought to be able to arrange something more modest without too much trouble. You will be taking your college boards pretty soon and if you do well on them that will help get you a good scholarship."

Andy sighed at the thought of the college boards and all the monkey business involved in applying for college entrance. Sometimes he thought it would be much easier just to find a job nearby after he graduated from high school.

"Why do I have to go to college?" he demanded suddenly. "I read somewhere just the other day that the big push is off college for everybody now. They're beginning to realize that a lot of people don't need a college degree at all; a good trade school is much better. How do I know that I *need* to go to college? It would be a hell of a lot cheaper not to."

"Don't be profane, Andrew," his mother said.

But Bob spoke to the point. "Well, what you say is true, Andy, but also you have to be awfully sure that what you really want to do *doesn't* require a college degree. What do you, as nearly as you can tell now, really want to do? How do you know that you *don't* need a degree?"

"I don't know, and I suppose that's the trouble," Andy replied. "Right now I *think* I'd like to teach, but I could change my mind."

"H'm," Bob observed, "that doesn't sound like a vocational school to me, but as you say, you might change your mind. Most students do change their minds several times before they get through school. That's healthy. I'd suggest you try two years of college and see how the wind blows then. Two years of college never hurt anybody; if you change your mind then, you can always take a couple of years of some trade, and no harm done. How about that?"

Andy could only agree.

Not too long after, he took the college boards and did so well that he surprised even himself. Then he sent out applications to three small colleges in the state, and also the University of Minnesota, for Bob's sake. He had graduated from there and felt that it would be good for Andy.

"You should spend a few years in the cities," he insisted. "You need some experience in a metropolitan community; and it has the added advantage of being far enough from home that you couldn't come running up here every weekend. But don't tell your mother I said that," he added with a grin.

At first Andy objected to the thought of going to Minnesota.

"Do you realize how many students there are at that school?" he howled. "The other day somebody told me there are 45,000, more or less. Can you imagine *me,* an Indian boy from northern Minnesota going there? I'd drown in that sea of people!"

"You don't join the whole University, you know," Bob said. "You are part of your own college, and you'd soon get used to it."

Andy was accepted by three of the four schools, including the University. His self-confidence was tremendously buoyed up, and he began to look forward to the next year. Soon he could even think about the University without shuddering. And finally to everyone's amazement, except Bob's, Andy chose the University. It seemed to offer the widest opportunities, and since he didn't know what he wanted to do, it seemed to make the most sense to go to a place where he would have a wide choice. Bob knew just how to set the wheels in motion to get student aid there. He promptly had Andy filling out a million blanks in duplicate, triplicate and quadruplicate.

It was going to cost a king's ransom, Andy thought to go to the University. Sometimes as he read the catalog, he couldn't imagine where all the money could possibly come from, but Bob talked confidently of national funds and state funds and special Indian scholarship funds until Andy's head whirled.

All too soon his three high-school years were gone, and spring had come again. Bob's discretionary fund had worked its last magic for him—a pair of handsome black dress shoes that he wore to the Senior Prom and then again on graduation night. It had also paid the rent for the cap and gown he wore.

He had done it at last! He was going to graduate! As he waited in the twilight for the first strains of "Pomp and Circumstance" to sound on the electric organ in the high-school auditorium, Andy began to sweat under his long gray gown. Yet he marched confidently up the steps that his rabbit head had bounced down so long ago. The class marched slowly, trying to keep in step with the music and look as dignified as possible; their feet made loud tramping noises in their unfamiliar new shoes as they moved down the long center aisle between the packed rows of families and friends. They climbed the steps to the platform and seated themselves in the chairs placed there. The faculty sat in seats reserved for them across the front of the auditorium.

In a row in front of the graduates sat the dignitaries of the town: the mayor, the superintendent of schools, the president of the Board of Education. Andy looked over their heads down into the audience. He spotted his family, with Johnny sitting next to his mother, and Harry and his sisters on her other side. Even one of his older brothers, through with college for the summer, had come home to see him graduate. Bob Underhill was with the faculty so Ann sat alone with Bobby and smiled at Andy. Mother and Johnny were looking at him, too, and he suddenly realized that probably those two and the Underhills cared more because he was finally graduating than any other people in the world.

His mother's black eyes, as they rested upon him in his cap and gown had a softness and a shine to them that he had never seen before, and the look on Johnny's face was as proud as though Andy were his own son, the one he had. . . .

The superintendent of schools stood up to open the graduation ceremonies, a minister gave the invocation, but Andy didn't hear a word. What was it Bob Underhill had said about his discretionary fund? "It's a kind of memorial for a son he used to have . . ."

Andy looked down at the shiny new shoes on his feet and smoothed the gray robe and touched the white tassel on his mortarboard. All those three years it had been Johnny! Who else could it possibly have been? How could he have been so stupid as not to guess? He looked down at Johnny again and this time caught his eye and they smiled at each other.

There were speeches and more speeches, most of them pretty boring, but finally they were done. The graduates all stood up, and as each one's name was called, he walked down alone to the front of the platform to be given his diploma and have his hand shaken by the president of the Board. By some miracle they had graduated from high school. Then they stood together to sing the school song for the last time as a class and went down to find their families.

Johnny was watching for Andy. He shook hands with him and said "Congratulations! You did it, Andy. I'm so proud!" and when he took his hand away, he had left something there. It was a crumpled twenty-dollar bill.

"Sorry I haven't more to give you, *gwe-we-zance!*" he said.

When Andy could control his voice, he said,

"Johnny, you have given me so much—for three years you have given me everything to keep me going, and I never guessed until tonight!"

thirteen

Summer began to wane in the northland, mornings were snappy and evenings chill. Andy's vacation job at the boatyard came to an end after Labor Day, and he had to go shopping for new clothes. He had saved all the money he could during the summer, so one day his friend, Pete, borrowed the family car and they drove over to Virginia. Andy had never paid much attention to the price of clothes before, so he was appalled when he saw the price tags and almost decided, there on the streets of Virginia, that he couldn't possibly afford to go to college.

Pete had just finished his first year at Bemidji State, so he was full of advice. He insisted that Andy buy the few clothes he would need for dress at school.

"Everybody wears jeans and turtlenecks on campus at the U. I hear, just the way we do at Bemidji, so that won't be a problem, but once in awhile you have to dress up for something, and you'd feel awful silly if you didn't have *something* besides blue jeans to wear. You need a sport jacket, a pair of slacks and a couple of good shirts. How about sweaters?"

"Mother knitted two for me last winter," said Andy. "One shirt will have to do. I can wash it out when it gets dirty. Let's get the kind I won't have to iron. I've got enough knitted sport shirts, too, at least for now."

They shopped until they found a light brown sport jacket on sale, and some plaid slacks to match. A gold shirt and a matching tie finished the outfit. Andy was pleased until he paid the staggering bill, which took all the money he had budgeted for clothes plus most of the twenty dollars Johnny had given him for graduation. He took his *first* brand-new clothes home for Mary Thunder to see with an awful feeling of guilt. All he could think of as he watched her admiring the jacket and running her hands appreciatively along the crease in the slacks, was his mother carrying water from the well for drinking and chopping a hole in Lake Vermilion ice in the winter for wash water. But he had just bought some expensive new clothes and was going to the University to live in a huge dormitory where he could have a hot shower every morning of his life.

Andy talked to Johnny about it in private that evening. "I think I'll take these clothes back, Johnny," he said. "I've been thinking, I don't have to have them to go to college. I've got a decent pair of brown jeans that I can wear with a dress shirt and a sweater if I have to go somewhere dressed up. I feel like a dog buying all this when they cost *so much* and my mother doesn't even have running water in the house. I never dreamed they'd cost all that money—just a few clothes."

"You didn't pay much for these clothes, *gwe-we-zance*,"

Johnny said. "I think you shopped well. That money wouldn't begin to pay for running water in Mary's house. You keep those clothes. They made her very happy. She'd feel bad if you didn't keep them. Someday when you're through school and earning money, you can buy running water for your mother."

With mixed feelings Andy followed Johnny's advice, packing his new clothes in the handsome brown suitcase the Underhills had given him for graduation. The overflow he put in corrugated boxes and tied them with cord. The next morning he would go to the University, so that evening he rowed over to the Major's to say goodbye and then followed the shore around to little East Two River and up to town to see the Underhills. His feelings were so mixed that he couldn't even try to put them into words.

The next morning he stood on the shore in front of his house and looked across at the blue hills and the gold-rimmed lake while he waited for Johnny to take him into the city. This was the end of something. September had come again, this time bringing a more drastic change than ever before. He had the strange feeling that the next time he stood there and looked across the lake he would see it with different eyes, that it would never look quite the same again.

A pall of silence hung over everything. The summer people were gone, their cabins closed for the season; the Indian children of the village were back in school. Ellen and Rosemary were busy in Junior High and Harry had been lucky enough to get a board and room job in Hibbing his first year in high school. Andy heard a very small sound behind him—Mary Thunder had come noiselessly from the house in her soft moccasins. At that moment the stillness was rent by the

94

snort of Johnny's old car roused to life, and it was a good thing. Andy ran to get his luggage, and his mother hurried back to the house to get a brown paper sack of lunch she had packed for them.

He started to peek inside, but Mother closed it quickly and smiled at him.

"Not now," she said. "Wait until noon when you stop to eat."

Andy got into the car beside Johnny; his mother at the last minute reached in and touched his cheek with her hand; and then they were off, chugging along the woodland road to the highway, through town, past the high school, and down the road to Ely, its edges lighted with sunflowers and goldenrod and wild asters, as it had been on the day Andy walked the rails to Ely with blisters on his feet. They rolled through Ely and took the undulating, roller-coaster road to Duluth.

Just outside the city, on the shore of Lake Superior, they stopped and sat on a rock while Andy opened the lunch his mother had given them. There were bannocks, of course, and two little jars of wild blueberries, and in the bottom of the sack, wrapped carefully and individually, two baked rabbit heads. DO NOT DROP, ANDY! she had lettered with black crayon on his. After they had eaten, he went across the highway to a little eating place to buy some hot coffee and two ice-cream cones.

It was the middle of the afternoon before they reached the campus and found the dormitory where Andy was to stay. As long as he lived he would never forget walking into the splendor of the lounge. Later he found out it was one of the old dorms and not nearly as elegant as some of the new ones. But it dazzled him that first time as he walked into it carrying his new suitcase, followed by Johnny, lumbering along with two cardboard cartons tied with string.

The room was full of boys and their parents. They more or less ignored Andy, and for that he was grateful. He went to the desk for the key to his room, and they went upstairs with his things. His roommate was already there, unpacking with the help of his mother. Andy knew his name was Martin Smith because a letter from the University had told him. Martin met him at the door with a cordial handshake and introduced his mother. Johnny was introduced and almost immediately left to look up the home of a friend where he had arranged to spend the night.

After Andy had gone downstairs with him and said a reluctant goodbye, he went back to unpack his belongings. Marty had a trunk and two suitcases, with an abundance of clothes. Andy's own new suitcase held up its head well, but the cartons were something else.

He was almost ashamed to unpack in front of Marty and his mother, who were trying to find room for everything in the dorm wardrobes and dressers. After Andy had put all his things away, there were still several empty drawers and lots of hooks left that were supposed to belong to him.

"Why don't you use these?" he asked. "I won't need them."

Marty started toward the drawers eagerly, but his mother intervened.

"Hold on, Marty," she said. "Andy doesn't need these places now, but when he brings his winter clothes down later in the fall he certainly will."

That left Andy with a question, what should he do? Save face and say, "Gee, that's right. I hadn't thought of that." Or be honest and say, "Thanks, Mrs. Smith, but this is it."

He decided on the latter. This was just one of the things he knew that he was going to have to face up to in college. It was humiliating to confess to Mrs. Smith that he had brought everything he owned with him this first trip, but it was better than putting up a big front and having Marty find out the truth as the year wore on.

She was very tactful about it and invited Andy to go out for dinner with them after the beds were made.

"I'll help you both," she offered gaily, "but let's hurry because I'm starving."

Andy had been, too, until she mentioned beds and began to rummage in a trunk for blankets. Then he simply felt sick. Blankets! Why hadn't Bob and Ann told him? But then he remembered, they wouldn't have known about it. Ann went to Moorhead State instead of the U., and Bob hadn't lived in a dorm; he'd stayed all four years with an aunt who lived in town. Now, what to do about blankets and a bedspread? Mrs. Smith was getting a plaid spread out, too.

He heard himself saying, "I guess I'll wait until later to make mine. I'll help make yours, Marty, while you finish unpacking."

Mrs. Smith's glance flitted lightly over his empty luggage.

"You forgot blankets, didn't you, Andy?" she asked gently.

Once more Andy felt compelled to tell her the truth.

"No, I didn't forget," he answered miserably. "I didn't know I had to bring 'em. I thought blankets would be supplied like the sheets and towels."

She started to speak, but this time it was Marty who stepped into the breach.

"Mom, I guess it's lucky you insisted on packing all those blankets." He turned to Andy, grinning. "She put in three heavy ones. You'd have thought I was going to the North Pole!"

His mother laughed. "Well, it's Minnesota—it's *cold* here in the winter. I 'spose it *was* silly, though. Who needs three blankets with modern heating?"

She came over to Andy's bed and laid a warm green blanket on it.

"Here, you use this one just as long as you need it, Andy," she said. "I don't wonder you missed it in the catalog. There's so much listed for freshmen to bring!"

She helped him put the sheets on, and they put the blanket on because nights are nippy in Minnesota in September. He'd make do without a bedspread for awhile. Then they walked out through the campus to Dinkytown to find a place to eat.

Andy was beginning to feel quite at home with both of them, but strangely enough he had the feeling that Marty felt tense about him, as though he were afraid he'd do or say the wrong thing. Andy could see that it was going to take awhile for them to be relaxed together. They had a good dinner, and then the boys drove Mrs. Smith out to the airport to catch a plane back to Illinois. She and Marty had come in Marty's car, so he could have it during the school year. Imagine having your own car! It was a blue Volkswagen bus that his mother and father had given him for graduation from high school. He had picked out that kind because he thought it would be handy for hauling luggage and books and passengers back and forth from the U.

Handy! To Andy it was unimagined luxury. He enjoyed the ride to the full.

fourteen

Andy was homesick his first few weeks at school, although he didn't know it. He felt lousy all the time, and once he went to the health service because he thought he must have a bug of some kind. The doctor checked him over but couldn't find anything actually wrong with him.

"There's a lot of it going around," he said with a friendly smile. "Always seems to hit the campus in the fall!"

He gave Andy some harmless pink pills to take, but they didn't help; nothing seemed to until a letter came from his mother reminding him that the wild rice was ready for harvest. She suggested that he come home for a ricing weekend and bring his roommate with him. She wanted to meet Marty. Andy perked up immediately after that.

He passed his mother's invitation along to Marty a little hesitantly because he wasn't sure how a city person would take to a house without any running water. But Marty accepted instantly; and when the weekend came, he and Andy drove up to Lake Vermilion in the VW bus.

Andy needn't have been afraid. Marty loved every minute

of the weekend. He rowed *Josie's Coat* around on the lake, and went over to Nett Lake to rice. Andy taught him how to bend the rice stalks over the canoe and shake the grains off into the bottom, and he was fascinated watching all the other parts of the rice harvesting process. But most of all he adored Andy's mother. Mary Thunder treated him with the same warm friendliness that she did every guest. Andy watched her with new appreciation. He admired her quiet dignity and the way she seemed not to notice Marty's brand-new car and his expensive clothes.

"*Things* just don't impress my mother much," he thought proudly, "but she does like Marty."

When it was time for them to go back to the city on Sunday evening and Marty was complaining because they had to leave, Mary Thunder handed him a little bag of popped wild rice and most impressive of all to Andy, a baked rabbit head!

"Come and see us again, Marty," she said. "Come back whenever you want to. You will always be welcome here."

Thinking about that rabbit head as they drove along, and remembering another rabbit head, Andy almost told Marty the story, but he couldn't quite bring himself to do it. Perhaps another time.

The visit home cured Andy's homesickness, but it also made him realize how much he missed having Indian people around. He had never been the only Indian before. Even in the lumber camp he had always had Johnny. In the dorm all the rest of the students were white, with a few blacks mixed in, and he felt alone. Marty had made many new friends, but Andy, with his Indian distrust of white people, held back. Even the guys who were especially nice to him gave him the feeling that maybe they were just tolerating him because he was Marty's roommate, and Marty was so popular.

Most of the boys went out for some kind of sport in their freshman year. Marty was on the freshman football squad, and during the season he was so busy that Andy seldom saw him.

"Why don't you go out for track, Andy?" Marty asked him one day. "You told me yourself that you kept winning meets for your track team in high school."

"I'd sure like to," Andy said regretfully, "but I can't take the time this year. I've got to keep my grades up or I won't even be coming back next year!"

After Marty went off to football practice Andy sat a long time at his desk just pondering the conversation. Such a pitifully small proportion of his people even graduated from high school, let alone college. Could he make it, or couldn't he? The old feeling of uncertainty that had plagued his first year in high school swept over him again. But in those days he had been able to turn to Bob and Ann to bolster him, but now he had to do it all alone.

There were days when the effort seemed almost too much; study, study, study all the time. Everybody else would be going to a party the weekend he had to study for a midterm or sit up all night finishing an important paper. And when he didn't have to study, he was out of money, waiting for a student aid check, and couldn't have asked a girl out, even if he'd had one to ask. He didn't have a date all that first term.

Finally fall term was over. Marty packed his VW bus with luggage and riders and headed for Illinois, promising to come a few days before New Year's to pick Andy up at the lake. When he said goodbye, his final instructions were,

"Hug Mary Thunder for me and tell her I'm coming!"

Andy took the bus up to Lake Vermilion, glad that finals were over and fairly certain that he had passed everything and would be going back for the winter term. He was surprised at how much he wanted to return, glad though he was to be going home for the holidays. His town, when they rolled into it at dusk, was shining with Christmas lights and covered with snow. Johnny had come to meet him, bringing Mary Thunder and his sisters, Ellen and Rosemary. Bob, Ann and Bobby were at the bus station, too, to celebrate his homecoming. They all went to the Underhills' and crowded into the little kitchen to drink hot chocolate and try Ann's Christmas cookies. Andy was home again, back with the people he loved, in the land that was his own. Later he, his mother, Johnny and the girls drove through the woods —silent in the snow—until they came to the white meadow where the lights from the clustered houses glowed like jewels.

Mary Thunder went in to light the lamp and stir the fire in the wood stove, and Johnny carried Andy's luggage in; but Andy and his sisters went down to the shore. The amber water of Lake Vermilion was frozen and covered with snow; but Johnny must have pulled *Josie's Coat* out before the water froze, because she was snugged bottom side up in the shelter of the dock, her brilliant stripes gleaming faintly through the snow. Andy made a mental note to find the old tarp he always used to cover her through the winter; the funny old boat was still his most precious possession. The door of the house opened, and he heard his mother calling,

"Come everybody, supper!"

Being at home that night with just the family and Johnny, who seemed like family, was perfect. Harry was still in Hibbing where he was in his first year of high school, but they expected him home for Christmas any minute. They sat at the table a long time that night, talking about the University and Andy's finals and Marty.

"No girl yet, Andy?" Johnny wanted to know.

Andy laughed. "No girl," he returned. "I'm looking for a pretty Indian girl, and I haven't seen one so far."

"No rush," said Johnny comfortably. "You take some advice from me. Don't settle for any girl who isn't as pretty as your mama!"

He winked broadly at Mary Thunder, and she smiled back at him.

"That's pretty poor advice, Andy," she assured him. "You'd better take your sisters as models, not your mother. Even when I was young I wasn't as pretty as they are, and now look at me—old and fat!"

"You're not old and fat!" Andy exclaimed indignantly.

"Amen! Amen!" Johnny seconded him. "There must be somethin' wrong with your mirror, Mary."

"I haven't had time to look in it lately," Mary said, laughing. "I've been so busy with Christmas, trying to get everything ready before you and Harry got home. Oh Andy, I'm so proud of him; he's doing so well in school this year!"

Ellen pouted. "Gee, Mom," she complained, "don't Rosie and me count at all around here anymore? All we hear is 'Andy and Harry, Andy and Harry' all the time!"

Rosemary giggled. "Don't pay any attention to her," she

said. "Her nose's out of joint, that's all. Andy, did you know the new Community House's done? We're going to have Christmas dinner there—the whole village."

"And we've got venison to take for our part," Ellen cried excitedly. "Johnny caught a buck."

"For goodness sakes, you don't *catch* a buck," Rosemary corrected her. "You *shoot* it!"

The next day everybody plunged into Christmas preparations. Johnny brought the venison in from the shed to thaw, and Mary got it ready for cooking. Harry arrived from Hibbing.

"Was I ever in luck!" he told them. "I got a ride from a man who was going all the way to Ely. Say, when are we gonna cut the Christmas tree, Andy?"

They went into the woods that afternoon and cut a big bushy balsam for the Community House and a little one for their living room. Ellen and Rosemary trimmed their own tree; then they went over to help the ladies trim the big one for the village. The girls were considered too big, this Christmas, to hang up their stockings, so they helped their mother fill baskets with cookies and little jars of jam made from wild berries that grew on the reservation. Then they carried them to Granny Kingfisher and Johnny's old cousin.

The celebration at the Community House went off perfectly. Each family brought something for the feast. Johnny's venison was delicious, everyone declared, and there was so much of it. The warm, cheerful room smelled of the roasted meat, and the delicate, indescribable fragrance of wild rice.

After dinner they all sat around the Christmas tree, and small gifts were passed out. Before the party was over, one of the boys brought out his guitar and played while they sang Christmas carols in Ojibway. Then families bundled up their dishes and their little children and went out into the night, still singing. Andy heard the sounds floating on the quiet, snow-filled air as he walked with his family toward their house.

"It was nice," said Mary Thunder, "having all of you home."

Andy heard the deep note of contentment in her voice, but he smiled to himself in the darkness as he noticed her backward glance at Johnny who was helping his cousin along in the snow.

A few days after Christmas, Andy's marks came in the mail. He had an *A* in history and a couple of *B*'s and one *C*, in math, of course. When Bob and Ann happened in that evening, Andy handed them to Bob without comment.

"Andy, I must say this is a surprise!" he exclaimed, handing them on to Ann. "I expected you to do well because I knew you were working hard, but I didn't really expect such grades this first term. This is something to live up to!"

"Whee!" Ann cried. "I'm so proud!"

"You should be," Andy grinned. "You had an awful lot to do with that *B* in English. If you hadn't helped me so much that first year in high school, I'd probably have flunked out because of freshman English. Aren't you upset with that *C* in math, Bob?"

"No way," said Bob. "That's very respectable for freshman math, Andy, when you consider that math isn't your meat. You'll never make an engineer, but then you don't want to be an engineer, do you?"

Andy exploded into laughter. "Me an engineer? Anything but that, almost. I haven't even thought very much about what I *do* want to do, yet, but it doesn't seem to worry me."

"Of course not," said Bob briskly. "You certainly don't need to worry your first year in college. What I want to know is didn't you do anything but study?"

"Yeah," Ann broke in. "What did you do for fun, Andy? Everybody needs to take time out for a *little* bit of fun."

Andy had to admit that he hadn't, at least not much. "I had to work hard for these marks," he said defensively. "I didn't have time *or* money for horsing around."

"That's nonsense," Bob chided gently. "You don't have to have much money to date a girl. There are dozens of things you can do for a date that don't cost more than the price of a Coke now and then. Aren't there any pretty girls on campus anymore? There were lots of them when I was there." He grinned at Ann.

"Sure, there're lots of pretty girls," Andy agreed, a little grudgingly, "but I haven't seen any Indian girls yet."

"Well, for heavens sake!" Bob exclaimed. "I'm sure they had an Indian Student Association or something like that. I can't remember what they called it, exactly. Strange they haven't gotten in touch with you."

Andy felt guilty because he vaguely remembered getting a postcard about a meeting of some such group and letting it get lost in the rubble on his desk. He'd have to hunt it up when he got back. Maybe there *were* more Indians around than he thought. Anyhow he'd have a little fun while he was home. He hunted up the girl he had dated occasionally the year before and took her skating on the lake in front of his house, and even double-dated at a movie with Pete and his girl one evening.

Then one morning just before New Year's, Andy was awakened by the raucous blast of a car horn outside his window. It had a familiar sound, loud and clear. While he struggled awake, he heard his mother calling from the door,

"Marty, come in! We've been expecting you!"

Andy pulled on his pants and ran out just in time to see Marty charge into the house and swoop up his mother on the way. He gave her a huge hug and a kiss on her shining black hair. Andy stopped short with his mouth literally hanging open; in all his life he had never done such a thing to his mother, and if he had tried he was sure he would have gotten a sharp cuff. But here was Mary Thunder, laughing like a girl and saying,

"Put me down, Marty, the very idea, but it's so *good* to see you again!"

She straightened her dress and smoothed her hair and turned primly to Andy.

"You bring in Marty's things, Andy, while I fix breakfast for him."

"Well!" Andy protested. "How about some breakfast for your son?"

Marty clapped him on the back and laughed. "*I* rate around here, boy. *I've* been away. You've been here eating your mother's great meals for two weeks, you lucky dog!" All of which earned him another delighted smile from Mary Thunder and a baked rabbit head for breakfast.

When Andy talked it over with his mother later he said,

"How come it didn't seem like Marty was taking liberties

with you? You'd think I'd gone out of my head if I were to pick you up and swing you around and hug you the way he did."

Mary Thunder smiled and answered, "I guess it's because that's the white man's way, Andy. Marty's a white man, so it's his way, and it seems quite natural for him to carry on like that, but it would seem very strange if you were to do it."

She was silent for a moment; and when she spoke again, he heard a touch of wistfulness in her voice.

"Indians don't speak their love much, with special love words and actions; and I think it is a good way, our way. We know that we care for each other without speaking the words, but sometimes I think maybe we lose a little because we are so—" she hesitated, fumbling for the right word.

Andy supplied it, "So austere, or maybe reserved?"

"That's it," his mother nodded. "I couldn't think of the right one. You'll be an English teacher yet." She laughed, and they didn't talk about it anymore.

Marty had a surprise in the back of his VW bus. He'd brought his favorite Christmas present along, a snowmobile from his mother and father. Everybody in the family had a marvelous time riding around in the snow the two days he was there. He took Ellen and Rosemary across the lake and up little East Two River to town, and Andy and Harry each had a turn driving it and taking their mother out. It was sad to have the holidays come to an end; Andy hated to start packing for the trip back to the University for winter term.

Bob and Ann came over their last night at home with a sign, neatly lettered in red, for Andy. It said,

"Don't get me wrong, And
great marks, but have some p
think I'm right, Marty?"

"Sure do," Marty agreed. "I was at h
out once in awhile. We're going to find us a
term, Bob. You watch!"

fifteen

Andy taped the sign up over his desk in the dorm as soon as they got back, and when he read in the paper a few days later that there would be an Indian powwow on Saturday night at St. Stephen's Church in Minneapolis, he decided to go. Marty had a date that night, and Andy didn't care to ask anyone else to go along, so he set out alone. He had never heard of St. Stephen's before, but a student who lived in Minneapolis told him which bus to take, the bus driver was cooperative, and miraculously he arrived at the right place at the right time.

He maneuvered through the group of young Indians milling around outside the door and walked into a long hallway full of more Indians. The girl who took his admission dollar suggested that he go into the room where they were serving supper and have some. Andy didn't really feel very hungry because he had eaten dinner at the dorm before he left, but as he walked down the hall the heavenly smell of bannocks frying, mingled with the fragrance of coffee and the delicate, subtle odor of wild rice cooking changed his mind. He sat down at a long table where people were eating, and a woman slid a paper plate filled with food in front of him. There were Indian families at the table and a few white families with children. The food wasn't quite up to Mary Thunder's standards, but it was Indian food and it tasted good. At first he was puzzled to hear people talking about the "good fry bread," but when someone offered him some from a basket, Andy knew it was what they called bannocks at home.

It made him feel good to be with Indian people, although he didn't know a soul in the place. When he had finished eating as much of everything as he could hold, he sat on at the table just looking around at the people, absorbing the warm glow of the copper-bronze faces, the clean, sculptured bone structure under the skin, the special blue-black sheen of the women's hair. These were his people, and he was at home with them; here he felt no stranger.

Several Indian men came up to speak to Andy, wanting to know where he came from and what he was doing in the Twin Cities. The older men nodded approval when he told them, but some of the younger ones had nothing at all to say. He couldn't tell whether they were just indifferent or really hostile.

The sound of drumming began to throb through the building, so he followed it to a gymnasium where the powwow was set up and about to begin. Spectators were sitting around the edge of the floor and up in the balcony. Andy went up there because he wanted to look down on the brilliant costumes. As he sat watching the dancers getting ready for the first dance, he saw a girl come out on the floor, dressed in a long white buckskin gown, fringed and beaded in the intricate flower patterns of the Chippewas—blues, reds, greens and gold. She wore white beaded moccasins on her feet, and her long black hair, shining in the bright lights, was parted in the middle and swept smoothly back into two sleek braids. He leaned over the balcony railing for a closer look and found himself staring straight down into her eyes, so like his mother's that he caught his breath. Mary Thunder must have looked like that when she was young. The girl half-smiled at him, but turned away when she saw he was a stranger.

The beat of the great drum was throbbing through the gym now, and the dancing had begun. The wailing chant of the singers rose above the beat as they sat, leaning forward, in a circle around the drum. Most of the singers were elderly Chippewas whose dancing days were done, but there were some young ones, too, who loved to sing the ancient songs of the tribe. Andy saw that there was another drum in the room with another circle of singers. The two groups would take turns drumming and chanting for the dancing during the long evening. Andy recognized some of the singers and dancers because he had seen them at powwows near home.

Andy leaned against the railing and stared down at the undulating line of dancing figures. He was aware that a white girl had come to take the seat next to him and was also leaning over the railing, but he paid no attention to her; he kept following the young girls and the women with his eyes, trying to find the beautiful one he had seen earlier. There she was! He thought she looked like an Indian princess among the other women as they moved with slow, graceful dignity through the rhythmic pattern of the dance.

The maidens of their tribal past must have looked like that, dancing in a clearing in the forest hundreds of years ago. How strange for them to be going through these ancient rituals in a smoke-filled gymnasium under hot electric lights with the drumbeats bouncing back from hard plaster walls!

Andy was pulled abruptly back to the present by the voice of the girl next to him.

"Nice, isn't it?"

"H'm-m-m," he agreed, not taking his eyes from the dance floor where the men and boys were now joining the women.

"Just like the birds," remarked the girl. "The females are always subtle and subdued in their plumage—the males brilliant and gaudy. Don't you think that's a good comparison?"

"I never thought of it just like that," Andy responded, turning to look at her for a moment, "but it figures, I guess."

Someday when he was through school and had paid off all his debts, he hoped he would have a gorgeous costume of his own. He would have a bristling roach on his head, a deerskin tunic beaded with Chippewa nature designs in brilliant colors, and beautiful medallions around his neck. Maybe someday he would even have a feather warbonnet, like the ones some of the older men were wearing.

The younger male dancers were moving now in a wild frenzy of motion. The bells on their ankles chimed an obligato to the roar of the drum. He could hardly bear to sit there passively with all that passionate turmoil going on below. He could hardly keep from leaping over the railing and dancing, too, even without a costume.

The white girl said, "Sometimes when I come to powwows, I think the city Indians living in this white man's world are venting their anger and frustration when the music gets like this. You're an Indian. What do you think?"

Andy was taken aback. He watched the dancing silently for a moment, and then he answered,

"Certainly I'm an Indian. But that doesn't mean I can answer your question; this is the first powwow I've been to in the city."

She accepted his answer without comment and asked,

"Why aren't you dancing? Don't you like to?"

"I'd like to dance," he replied, a little irritably, "but the fact is I don't have a costume; I don't have money to buy one, either; and I'm too busy going to school to dance even if I did have one."

"Oh? Where do you go?" she asked. "I'm a student, too. I'm a freshman at the University."

"So am I," Andy nodded, and introduced himself.

"I'm Angela Chester from Stillwater," she said. "I like your name. I think real Indian names are exciting."

Now Andy asked a question, "What brings you to a powwow over here all by yourself?"

"I'm not alone," Angela assured him. "See that girl down there in the gorgeous white buckskin dress? I came with her."

"You did!" Andy exclaimed. "What's her name? How do you happen to know her?"

"One question at a time!" Angela laughed. "Yes, I did come with her, or rather she came with me in my car. Her name is Tamara Jay, and I happen to know her because she's my roommate and we're both training to be social workers.

We're in the Social Work Associates program."

"I know about that," Andy told her. "In fact I almost decided to go in for it myself, but I changed my mind."

"Oh, that's too bad. What did you change your mind to?" Angela asked.

"I haven't really decided yet," Andy answered. "Teaching maybe."

Angela made a disappointed little sound. "Social work's so much more exciting," she said. "If you really want to get with it these days, you almost have to have a social-work background."

Andy shifted his position so he could see Tamara a little better, while he went on talking to Angela.

"What makes you think teachers aren't with it?" he demanded. "I can't think of a better place than a school to work with minorities."

Angela whirled from watching the dancers to stare at him.

"Well!" she exclaimed, "that's not the way I see it. The minority kids get the poorest education of all. The *good* teachers won't teach in their schools. I suppose it's your business, but I think you'd just be wasting your time trying to be a one-man reform team."

"I think you're all wrong about the teachers," Andy snapped. "I'll bet there's lots of good ones who teach in poverty-area schools and do a swell job. If you take an attitude like that, you won't make much of a social worker."

Angela gave him a piercing look.

"Say, where did you come from, anyway? You aren't a *reservation* Indian are you?"

Irked as he was, Andy had to laugh.

"Yes, as a matter of fact I am," he assured her. "Member of the Bois Forte Band, fresh off the Lake Vermilion Reservation this fall. What's so terrible about that?"

"Well," Angela said apologetically, "there's nothing terrible about *being* a reservation Indian, of course, but it's the reservation itself that's so terrible. Herding all you Indians together on reservations was the worst, positively the *worst,* thing we white people ever did!"

Andy was torn between annoyance at her patronizing manner, and appreciation of her very real distress. But he knew that the problems she had brought up would not be settled that night. The powwow was ending; people had begun to stream out of the gym. He wanted to go down with Angela and be introduced to Tamara.

"OK, Angela," he said hastily, "let's put it all together another time. I want to meet your roommate now."

Angela introduced him to Tamara and then invited him to ride back to the campus with them in her red Toyota.

"I'm certainly glad to find that there is at least one Indian female on campus," Andy told her. "I had begun to think there weren't any, male *or* female."

Tamara smiled up at him. "Well, it's bad, but it's not that bad," she said. "Didn't you get the card about the American Indian Student Association? I got roped into addressing them to new Indians on campus the first week I was here, and I remember seeing your name on the list. But you never turned up."

Andy flushed; she was waiting for an answer—he had to say something. Just mumbling or letting it pass wouldn't do. He decided to tell her the truth.

"Well," he drawled, "I do remember seeing a card about

some Indian group or other, but it must have gotten lost under the junk on my desk and never came to light again."

He decided on a bold tactic. "When you never saw me, why didn't you come looking?"

"Yes, why didn't I?" She laughed. "I'll let you know when we have the next meeting, and you *come* this time, Mr. Andrew Thunder."

"You couldn't keep me away!" Andy promised.

Angela drove around by his dorm, and they sat out in front talking for a while longer. Tamara wanted to know about his family and Lake Vermilion. Andy discovered that she knew very little about Indian reservations and what life was like on one. She came from a small town in the Upper Peninsula of Michigan where her father managed a farm-implement business. He and her mother had both been born on a reservation, but Tamara and her brother and sister had never lived there.

"Sometimes I almost wish I *had* lived on the reservation, at least for a few years while I was in high school," she mused. "I think it would help me now to understand what reservation Indians face when they move into a big city. Urban Indian problems are going to be my field in social work."

"Well, I don't know about that," Andy said uncertainly. "I think you were darned lucky to go to town schools all the way through. It's awful hard to make the change when you get to high school."

All of a sudden he was spilling out the whole story of his high school debacle: his year at Angleworm Lake, the disastrous summer, his fight with Bad Bill, and winding up with his return to school.

"And so here I am," he finished, "but it wasn't easy!"

The girls had listened in fascinated silence, except for little sympathetic noises once in awhile.

"What a terrific story," Tamara sighed when he was through.

"I can't imagine how you get along in school without any financial help from home," marveled Angela.

Andy looked at her clothes and her shiny Toyota.

"It's hard," he said briefly. "But I have scholarships and student aid, of course, or I couldn't do it. Maybe I'll try for a job spring term if my marks hold up this term. I sure do need one!"

"Why don't you try living off campus next year? I'm going to; it's cheaper," said Tamara.

"I've thought of it," Andy agreed, "and I'd really like to, but my mom objects, thinks I wouldn't eat properly."

They all laughed, and Tamara said, "Mine too, but I think I've got her talked into it, almost. Angie's going to live at the Pi Phi house next year, so it'll be a good time for me to do it."

"Yeah," Andy said, "I'm going to lose my roommate, too. Marty's going to move into his fraternity house. I'd like to get a cheap apartment so I can cook my own meals."

"Fry bread, wild rice—", Tamara murmured ecstatically. "You'll never know how hungry I get for them while I'm away from home. My mouth waters just thinking about Indian food."

"What do you know about it, you city Indian, you?" Andy demanded.

"Don't get me wrong," Tamara smiled. "My mom cooks great fry bread! I grew up on it."

"I like Indian food, too, you know," Angela spoke up. "Don't forget me, when you both begin cooking next year."

"You'll get a bite or two every now and then; and you can always get some at the Indian Center," Tamara reminded her. She turned to Andy, "By the way, would you like to go over there with us sometime when you aren't loaded with work? It's a place in Minneapolis where a lot of Indian kids hang out after school and at night."

"Sure," Andy said, getting out of the car. "What goes on there?"

"All sorts of stuff," Tamara replied. "Arts, crafts, games. After school there're always a couple of tutors around to help kids who aren't doing so well in reading, math, etcetera. It's the busiest place!"

"Sounds great!" Andy said. "Where do the kids come from?"

"Mostly from the neighborhoods around the Center," Tamara answered. "Most of them poor. Lots of them just want a good listener; that's where we volunteers come in. The paid staff is too small to have time for much of that."

"Sometimes I've had a girl stop right in the middle of beading a pair of moccasins," Angela said, "and start spilling out her troubles to me. If it doesn't seem too serious, I try to help her work it out myself; but if I see it's out of my league, I take her to a pro."

"You'd better come over and see for yourself," Tamara urged. "I'll bet you haven't seen very much of the way most Indians live in the city."

"Not very much," Andy agreed, "All I know is how most Indians live on the reservation!"

The girls laughed at that, although Andy hadn't meant it to be funny.

"Give me your phone number at the dorm, and I'll give you a buzz the next time we go over," Tamara suggested. "I'll give you my number, too."

Then the girls drove off; and Andy went up to his room and stared thoughtfully at Bob's reminder over his desk while he undressed. He wrote Tamara's phone number in one corner and went to bed, feeling anything but dull.

sixteen

Andy didn't wait for Tamara to call him; he called her one night soon after the powwow, and they went for a walk along the river bluffs with the thermometer ten below zero and a full moon sailing over the frozen river. They raced each other along the path to keep warm and ended the walk in a warm little shop where they thawed out with a pot of hot coffee. Andy smiled to himself, remembering what Bob had said about the price of a date.

"It was so much fun, Andy. Let's do it again!" she said when he left her at her dorm.

After that night the evening walk came to be a regular thing. Sometimes they went right after dinner and studied later; sometimes they went late at night after a long evening in the library. Now and then Angela went with them, but more often they went alone. During those walks Andy felt that he and Tamara grew to know each other very well.

Sometimes instead of walking in the evening, they went to the Indian Student Association meetings on campus, where Andy finally made friends with some of the "invisible" Indians that he had insisted weren't there. In the spring there were picnics and bike hikes; he enjoyed it all as a break from studying. Of course he met other girls, too, but none that he felt like asking for a date. He found himself comparing each one with Tamara, and none compared favorably. All her friends called her Tam or Tammy, but Andy called her Tamara. He thought it suited her.

And then one spring evening Tamara talked Andy into going with her to the Indian Center. After he saw the poverty area where the Center was located, he knew exactly how she felt when she grieved over the people who lived there. There were a few poor whites and blacks, but most of the residents were Indians. He doubted whether their desolate homes were any worse than many on the reservations; but the surroundings were so bad that they seemed much worse. You couldn't look away from the run-down dwellings and see a beautiful lake, rolling meadows and cool, dark woods. It was all squalor and unkempt dooryards and rubbish lying around, and little children romping—lovely, dark-eyed children, with no grass to romp on.

Andy wondered what the forlorn brick "flats" were like inside.

"If you really want to know, I'll take you to visit some friends of mine," Tamara offered.

Andy hesitated. "Wouldn't they think I was snooping?" he asked. "They know you, but they don't know me at all. Maybe they'd resent me."

"You're an Indian, aren't you?" Tamara retorted crisply. "It all depends on how you react to them. If they think you

122

feel you're better than they are, they'll resent it; but if you're just natural and everyday and act the way you would if you were going into Granny Kingfisher's house in your own village, they'll like you. In fact, I'm going to take you to visit an old woman who is very like Granny, the way you described her to me." She smiled at him and finished, "Just be yourself, Andy, and don't worry."

Andy was still a little apprehensive as they walked a block or two down the street from the Center and came to a row of what had obviously been elegant town houses in another day. Tamara rapped on a door, and an old woman drew the curtain aside just far enough to peek out. When she recognized Tamara, she came to let them in. There was a long, uncarpeted hall lit by one bare light bulb. The old woman, leaning heavily on a cane, went before them to her door and stood aside for them to enter. Limping around the cluttered room to clear off chairs for them, she did remind Andy a great deal of Granny Kingfisher.

They chatted awhile in air so foul and oppressive that Andy thought he would suffocate if he didn't get outdoors soon. There were odors of people and stale cooking smells, and the unmistakable smell of a cat. In a moment the cat appeared from under a broken-down sofa and jumped up on Mrs. Beaudoin's lap.

"Goldie don't look so thrifty," the old woman sighed, stroking the cat's shabby fur with swollen arthritic fingers. "She want to go out, but I don't let her. Somebody'd be sure to steal her offen me, and she's all I got for company. I can't get out the way I used to."

There was a scuffling sound in a dark corner of the room,

123

and Goldie, suddenly coming to life, leaped down and streaked across the floor toward it.

"That dratted rat agin!" Mrs. Beaudoin exclaimed. "Don't know what I'd do without Goldie to go after it. She don't never catch it, but she keeps it out of the room most of the time. When the grandchildren are here, I don't have no need to worry that it will bite them."

She must have noticed the shiver that Andy couldn't hide, because she said,

"Tamara, your friend here don't know rats bite little kids. Did you hear about the rat-bite the Edmond baby got the other day?"

"Oh no! Not the new one!" Tamara exclaimed.

"Yup, the danged rat jumped right into the crib when Mary was out hangin' clothes and bit the baby's little finger 'most off. Would have if Mary hadn't heard the child cryin' and come runnin' in."

Andy looked around the room to help him forget the gruesome story. He thought it was one of the most forsaken-looking places he had ever seen. Mrs. Beaudoin had just one room to eat and sleep and live in. There was a double bed in one corner, some open shelves on the wall to hold what little food she had, and a few dishes and pots. She did have a little old refrigerator, a battered sink with rusty water dripping out of a faucet, and a two-burner gas plate.

"At least she has running water," Andy thought, remembering the houses at home.

Tamara was talking to Mrs. Beaudoin. "Is Fred staying at home these days?" she asked.

The old woman's face darkened. "I ain't seen him in a

month," she replied. "Last I heard he got fired from his job and was drug out to the Workhouse for bein' drunk agin. Funny thing they arrested him. My neighbor read in the paper they ain't supposed to do that no more. Drunk folks is supposed to be sick, not criminals, the docs say."

"I know," Tamara said gently. "That is true. I'll check on him for you if you like, and now Andy, I think we'd better be going. It's past your bedtime, isn't it, Mrs. Beaudoin?"

Everybody laughed, a little hollowly, it seemed to Andy, and he and Tamara went out into the night. They walked in silence back to the Indian Center because Andy was too overwhelmed to speak. Angela was there having a cup of coffee and a doughnut, talking with a group of young Indians. Andy was introduced, and she gave him coffee and passed the doughnuts. It revived him a little, and finally he began to talk about what he had just seen.

"Mrs. Beaudoin?" said one of the men. "Hell, you ain't seen nothin' yet. Tam's breakin' you in easy. Just picture a family with two grownups and a lot of kids livin' in a place like that. She's only got herself and that gosh-awful cat."

"And Fred," Tamara put in. "She told me Fred got picked up again. Anybody know if he's still in the Workhouse? I told her I'd check. She's heard the new rule that alcoholics are supposed to be taken somewhere and dried out—not arrested. She's upset, and I don't blame her."

"The fuzz probably framed him and clapped a misdemeanor on him," someone said. "He's given them so much trouble; they hate him."

"Too bad we didn't get to him first, poor guy," remarked a man named Mike. "Ain't it a shame they don't try to do somethin' for boozers like him? He oughta be sent some-place for the cure."

He looked around at Angie, and lowered his voice. "But that's the white man for you; the way they operate. If it's gonna cost them much money, they don't do it. Each time Fred's in the Workhouse he comes out worse'n he went in, it seems."

"What d'you mean, 'too bad we didn't get to him first'?" Andy asked.

"Another cup of coffee all around," suggested Mike, who worked full time on the Center staff. Then they told Andy about the patrol they had set up to make the rounds of the area. Weekend and holiday nights some of them took turns driving up and down the streets, on a regular beat, trying to keep people from getting into trouble with police. It had been going on for some time and was pretty effective.

"Kind of like preventive medicine," explained Mike. "If we see somebody who's had too much to drink, we pick him up in the car and take him home where his own folks can take care of him. Saves a lot of 'em from being thrown into the drunk tank down at the courthouse and probably gettin' a Workhouse sentence."

"Lately we been takin' a teenager along with an adult—mostly weekend nights. They help us a lot with the kids," someone else said. "A teenager can spot one of his buddies a block away, and if he's in trouble, we move in fast."

"Yeah, and they help with the parties, too," another man observed. "We hear from them where there's goin' to be a party that's apt to get outta hand, and we get there and warn them to put the lid on before a neighbor calls the cops.

126

When it's Indian kids, the fuzz usually swing the clubs first and ask questions later."

"How about me going along some night?" Andy asked. "I haven't got a car, but I'd sure like to ride along with one of you."

"Sure thing," Mike agreed quickly. "How about next weekend? My regular buddy's going to be out of town—glad to have you."

So when the weekend came, Andy went on patrol. Nothing very exciting happened. They picked up a pair of drunks and put them in the back seat, and they stopped a gang fight between some teenagers just before a police squad car cruised by. They picked up an old woman who had fallen in the street on her way to the grocery store, did her shopping for her, and took her home.

Andy asked how the cops felt about the Indian patrols.

"Not so bad now," Mike told him. "At first they didn't think much of the whole idea. Wondered what we were up to, I guess, but lately they seem to have changed their minds. We save them quite a bit of time, and save our folks a lotta busted heads!"

They cruised around, up and down the dark, dreary streets. On one corner a crowd of noisy teenagers were whooping it up, and Mike told them to cool it and get on home; it was past curfew time for some of the younger ones.

"What're we going to do with the guys in the back seat?" Andy wanted to know.

"We'll drop them off where they live," Mike said. "Barney lives just around the corner and down the block, and say, you know the other one. He's Fred Beaudoin."

"Oh?" Andy said. "Well, I don't know him, exactly, but of course I met his mother the other night. I thought he was in the Workhouse."

"Just out," Mike said. "Good old Fred, up to his old tricks. He just gets dried out, and he's back on the bottle again."

"From what his mother said, he's had one Workhouse stretch after another. Certainly doesn't seem to do him much good," Andy remarked. "Did anybody ever try to get some real therapy for him at one of those hospitals where they have alcoholism units?"

"Nope, not that I know of," Mike answered. "Those places cost *money,* man, or didn't you know? Most of them are for whites with plenty of bread. Ain't that the way with everything?"

"I don't know," Andy mused. "An Indian guy from up home came down to the city to one of them—was gone a couple of months and came home OK. He was poor enough, an alcoholic all his life, pretty near. Somebody must have worked it out for him."

Mike shrugged, "Must have had a rich uncle," he said carelessly. "We'll get rid of Barney here."

He pulled in to the curb in front of a forlorn old frame house. They got out and together helped Barney out of the car and up the sagging steps. A woman came to the door at Mike's rap and accepted him without comment. "Thanks," she tossed back over her shoulder as she guided Barney down the dark hallway.

"Thanks for nothing," Mike observed sardonically. "If he was mine, I don't know if I'd *want* him back! Now let's take Fred back to his mama."

They drove around to the place. Mrs. Beaudoin was up, late as it was. She limped to the door to let them in, and the look of sorrow mingled with anger that she turned on her son struck at Andy. Fred slumped on the bed, and instantly fell asleep.

"Where did you find him this time?" Mrs. Beaudoin asked wearily, putting her teakettle on to boil. "You'll have a cup of tea?"

They nodded, and Mike answered her first question, "Lying in the gutter in front of the bar," he said briefly. "I guess they kicked him out."

"More than likely," his mother sighed. "He only got out of the Workhouse yesterday."

As Andy watched her dark, wrinkled face, all the anger suddenly went out of it, leaving only the sorrow.

"He ain't a *bad* boy," she murmured sadly as though to reassure herself. "He ain't never committed no crime—just been a nuisance when he's drunk. When he's sober, you couldn't find no nicer fella."

The teakettle had begun to sing, and she turned to the stove to brew the tea.

"Yeah, that's right," Mike whispered to Andy, grinning. "Fred's a great guy, all right; if you can ever catch him sober, that is!"

Andy didn't find the remark amusing. His mind flashed back to the summer when he had begun to drink with Kenny, and the night of his drunken brawl with Bad Bill. He had failed to see humor in drunk jokes ever since.

Mrs. Beaudoin brought them tea; they drank it and talked a little longer before they left. Then she stood in the doorway of her room and watched them go. On a sudden impulse Andy turned back to her and took her hand.

"Don't be discouraged," he said softly. "Maybe I can find some way to help him."

The old woman looked up at him gratefully, but shook her head.

"Thanks son," she said, "but I don't think there's nothin' nobody can do for my Fred. He's forty years old and he's been drinkin' all his life, it seems to me."

Andy gave her a pat on the shoulder and said, "Well, I'll try, anyhow."

He ran out after Mike, and they drove over to the dorm.

"Thanks a lot for bringing me way over here," Andy said, standing beside the car for a minute. "This has been quite a deal; I've learned something, all right."

"Thank *you* for giving me a hand," Mike answered. "You didn't see too much action tonight, but I'll be callin' you again."

He started to drive away but slammed on the brakes, leaned out the window, and called to Andy, who was almost inside the door,

"Andy, don't get me wrong. I'm not all that tough about drunks. You maybe thought I was pretty cynical about Fred and Barney."

Andy raised his arm in a goodbye gesture. "No way, man, no way!" he assured him. "You wouldn't keep lugging them home night after night if you were."

seventeen

Mike did call Andy a couple of weeks later to ask if he could take time to go to court on Thursday morning. Fred Beaudoin had been accused of robbing a gas station, and they were needed as witnesses. He would explain later. Andy skipped a class and went.

"Poor guy," said Mike as they drove along toward the Courthouse, "he's really a no-good punk, but I don't like him to be accused of something he couldn't possibly have done."

Mike slowed up for bridge traffic and went on,

"He and another guy were supposed to have held up a gas station at eleven o'clock the night you patrolled with me and we picked him up drunk in front of the bar. Now you probably wouldn't remember the exact time we picked him up, but I do because I'm used to thinking about the time things happen when I'm on patrol; you never know when it's gonna come in handy. I looked at my watch when we put him in the car and it was 10:15. We helped the old lady after that

131

and cruised around for awhile before we got to Barney's house and let him out. Then we got to Fred's place and went in; it must have been close to 11:15."

"Uh-huh," Andy agreed, "and Mrs. Beaudoin made tea for us and we must have talked to her for at least ten minutes after. Then you took me home, and it was midnight when I got into my room. I remember thinking it was pretty late to call Tamara, but I did, anyhow."

Mike nodded, looking around for a place to park at the Courthouse.

"Well, we were with Fred every minute from 10:15 to about 11:30 when we left their place, so it was absolutely impossible for him to be sticking up a gas station at 11:00," he said. "Lucky for him we picked him up that night."

"Yeah," said Andy doubtfully, "but maybe the judge won't believe us. I don't know how it is here; but where I come from Indians don't get justice very easy in the white man's court."

Somebody pulled out of a parking place, so Mike scooted into it. "It isn't easy," he admitted, "but there'll be one of our lawyers with Fred this morning, and with us as witnesses we just may be lucky enough to get him released at the preliminary hearing."

Andy dug a couple of dimes out of his pocket and put them in the meter. They walked into the Courthouse, and Andy asked curiously,

"How did Fred get a lawyer? It costs so much, and they seem so poor."

"Poor as Job's turkey," Mike nodded, "but this lawyer won't cost them much, if anything. A few years ago some lawyers in town got a dose of guilty conscience about us Indians, I guess, because when our organization asked for legal help they came through, and now we got a bunch of them who help when sombody gets hauled into court for somethin'. It started out small with just three or four, but now we've got around thirty on call, I think."

"Who pays 'em?" Andy persisted. "Lawyers' fees are high."

"These people only ask what Indians can afford to pay; and if they're really down and out, they don't have to pay anything."

Andy followed Mike through the wide doors into the courtroom and looked around curiously. He saw Fred Beaudoin sitting in front at a table with another man. Fred seemed to be quite sober and also quite chastened, dressed in a clean pair of pants with a freshly ironed shirt and a necktie. Mrs. Beaudoin was sitting unhappily in a row of seats in back of him, and Andy went over to speak to her. Just then Tamara came into the courtroom and slipped into the seat next to her. Andy was surprised to see her because she had said she couldn't come; she had English class. She smiled at him and whispered,

"I decided to skip English this morning and come over. I knew Mrs. Beaudoin would be here and would be scared, all alone."

She squeezed the old lady's hand and a quick smile lighted the wrinkled face. Andy joined Mike and was introduced to Fred's lawyer, who told them the kind of questions to expect and gave them a few simple suggestions. Then the judge came in from his chambers, and everyone stood for a moment. Andy began to feel very tense as the hearing began.

133

This was his first experience with the law. The lawyer addressed the court and gave a brief account of his client's activities the evening of the burglary, then asked to present his two witnesses.

Mike spoke first and told of his evening patrol duties and what had happened the particular evening in question. Then Andy was called to the witness stand. As he was sworn in, he looked down at the small group of people in front of him. Tamara must have sensed his tension because she smiled at him. Andy found nothing but raw fear in Mrs. Beaudoin's face as she looked at him; then his eyes came to rest on Fred. Although Andy had never seen him sober before, and very briefly when drunk, he was sure that Fred was terribly frightened. Perhaps for the first time in his life, he realized how helpless he was. He had been completely unaware of what had gone on that night when he was supposed to have committed a serious crime. As far as he knew, he *might* have been involved; he could not protect himself against anyone who might choose to accuse him, rightly or wrongly.

The words he had spoken to Fred's mother that night came into Andy's mind: "Maybe I can find some way to help him."

Andy straightened his shoulders and looked directly into the lawyer's eyes as he answered the questions put to him. Yes, he understood that Fred was being accused of the gas station holdup because he had been seen in the neighborhood earlier that evening by someone who thought he looked like one of the burglars. Yes, he understood that Fred was an alcoholic and not considered a stable character. Yes, he had been patrolling with Mike that night. Was it possible that the hour they picked Fred up was 11:15 instead of 10:15 as Mike recalled it? No, that wasn't possible, and Andy went into the details briefly but firmly.

"And," he wound up his testimony, "I looked at my watch when I got into my room and decided to call my girl, even though it was midnight. She wasn't called as a witness because she wasn't with us, but she's here this morning. You can swear her in if you don't believe me, and she will tell you it was true."

"That won't be necessary," said the judge. "The accused will be released because the court finds no possibility of his involvement in the crime of which he was suspected. The hearing is dismissed."

"Tamara, what are we going to do about Fred?" Andy demanded. They had talked to Fred and his lawyer after the hearing, had told Mrs. Beaudoin how happy they were about the dismissal, and now the Beaudoins were on their way home with Mike in his car. Tamara and Andy were taking the bus back to the U.

For once Tamara had no answer. "I don't know," she said doubtfully. "I feel a little like his mother does, I guess. Maybe after all these years there isn't much that *can* be done for him, especially without money."

Andy looked at her in amazement. It was the first time since he had known her that she hadn't been able to come up with some solution to a problem.

"I don't agree with you," he said finally. "There must be someplace in a city as big as Minneapolis where people like Fred can be helped, and there must also be someplace where I can find out about it."

They rode along in silence for awhile, and then Tamara said, still uncertainly, "Maybe they would know at the School of Social Work at the U. I could ask one of my professors."

"No, I'll take care of it," Andy heard himself saying, to his surprise. "I think I'll call General Hospital. They must know."

He did, as soon as he got back to his dorm. He dialed the number, told the person who answered what his problem was and was switched to the detoxification center. As concisely and quickly as possible, he told the man on the phone what he wanted.

"Is he drunk now?" came the question.

"No, he isn't," said Andy. "At least I don't think he is; he wasn't when I last saw him, about forty-five minutes ago."

The man sighed, "Well," he said, "I'd like to think he's still sober, and if he is, you should get him right over to the Indian Neighborhood Club. I'll give you the address. Just a minute while I check it."

He was back at the phone immediately. "That's the right one," he said. "And it's the best place I can think of for you to take this man. I've seen them take people in over there who've been in detox here and seemed absolutely hopeless. They're scared to death of this all-white setup of ours, but when they get into this Indian plan, you almost have to call what happens a miracle. When we ask what in heaven's name they do to a guy, they just shrug and say,

"Well, he knows we're concerned about him, and we just keep plugging away and give him an awful lot of plain, old-fashioned *love*."

"How much does it cost?" Andy asked fearfully. "There isn't any money."

"That's the beauty of it," the man replied. "It doesn't cost the patient a cent."

Andy sighed with relief, thanked him and in a minute was talking to Mike. Mike said he would pick Fred up at his house, meet Andy at his dorm and take them both to the Indian Neighborhood Club. Then Andy called the Club, fortunately got the director immediately, gave him a brief picture of the situation and was told to come right over. Next he called Tamara.

"Do you want me to go with you?" she wanted to know. "If you do, I can cut another class, I guess."

"No, I'll do this alone," said Andy. "Mike will be there, too. Thanks a lot anyhow, Tamara. I'll see you tonight and tell you all about it."

That evening Andy did tell her about it. He had found the director to be a wonderful person. There had been a chance to talk privately with him about Fred, and when Mr. LeMon heard that Fred didn't have a good place to stay in his mother's crowded little room, he suggested that he remain in the Club for awhile. Mr. LeMon told Andy they would use Fred around the Club as a cook and handyman, and that he would have the best one-to-one partner available among their recovered members.

"Poor guy," Mr. LeMon had said, "he's probably felt all his life that he isn't any good, that he doesn't amount to anything. And I'm sure that inside he feels that way about all Indians. We'll have to help him get over that before he'll get over his heavy drinking."

"Was Fred happy when you left him?" Tamara asked. "Do you really think he wanted to stay?"

Andy laughed. "He had a clean room, a bed with clean

sheets all to himself, and the men were having snacks in the kitchen when we left. The last thing I heard was somebody telling him they'd be singing Indian songs tonight and he could take a turn beating the drum."

"I'm so glad," sighed Tamara. "Andy, you did a marvelous job, getting him taken care of like that. I just can't believe it, all in such a short time. Does his mother know about it? Maybe Angela would take us over there tonight so you could tell her. She'll be so happy."

"She knows; Mike promised to stop by and tell her," Andy answered. "I'd like to see her myself tonight, but I've spent so much time with Fred today that I've got to hit the books for that exam coming up tomorrow. Let's get going, Tamara."

eighteen

Finals week hit the campus like a violent spring storm. Everyone was studying madly when the letter came from Andy's mother.

"I want to meet Tamara," she began abruptly. "Couldn't she come home with you for a few days before she goes to Michigan? I'd like Marty to come, of course, and how about that girl you call Angie? Johnny has a surprise for you."

Andy showed the letter to Tamara first.

"Oh Andy, I'd *love* to go!" she exclaimed. "But first I have to move all my stuff to the house where I'm going to stay next fall. Did I tell you that our landlady said we could store things in a basement room this summer?"

"Nope," said Andy. "Last I heard you had to pack it all up and take it home to Michigan. I'll help you move. Gee, aren't you in luck! I'm kind of discouraged about finding a place; the one I looked at yesterday was nice, but the price is so high I couldn't even think about it. Guess I'll have to come back early in September and look some more."

Marty was going to summer session for a couple of courses he couldn't get during the year, so he didn't plan to go home until August. He was delighted to accept Mary Thunder's invitation. Angela was going, too, though she was busy moving her things over to the Pi Phi house. They all studied and helped each other pack in their spare time, but Andy snatched an hour to drop in on Fred one evening.

"They're *nice* to me here," he told Andy, "I work around the place every day, and I get paid for it, too!"

Before Andy left, Fred told him about an old violin he owned and had held onto for years.

"Many's the time I almost hocked it for money to buy booze, but somethin' always told me to hang onto it," he said. "I used to fiddle and call square dances up in the country," he explained, "but then I got so I was under the influence so much that I couldn't anymore. It's busted now, but Mr. LeMon is gonna get me the stuff I need to fix it, and you just watch; in a little while I'll be fiddlin' again."

Andy was so thrilled at the change in Fred that he dashed over to see Mrs. Beaudoin.

"Fred's getting along just great," he told her.

"I know." She beamed at him. "Mike come by and took me over to see him yesterday. And do you know what he told me? He said when he's got a real job, he's gonna save his money and git us a real nice apartment with a bedroom, a real bedroom, and I can sleep in it. Just think, I'm gonna have a bedroom all for myself to sleep in!"

Her eyes were bright with hope, and Andy thought to himself,

What if the dream doesn't come true? What if Fred falls

off the wagon? I wish I had the money to get that bedroom for her!

But then he knew that it had to be Fred who made the dream come true for his mother. He talked it over with Tamara later.

"You see," she said, "it's the way I told you. Our people here need so much, especially the old ones and the little children. You're so smart, Andy. You really have the touch; you have so much to give them. Stay here in the city after you graduate."

Andy waited a minute before he answered her, and then he said calmly,

"I really don't know now, Tamara. There's another year before I need to think much about it."

It was hard for Andy to realize that his freshman year was over when he stowed his luggage in Marty's VW and the four of them headed north.

"What in the world is your mother going to do with all of us in your house?" Angela suddenly demanded. "Isn't it quite small?"

Andy laughed. "Small yes, Angie; but don't worry. Mom has made that house stretch for a awful lot of folks in her day. Imagine what it was like when all of us kids were at home! I got a letter from her yesterday, and she said for us all to pray for a dry spell because Marty and I will probably have to sleep out in the yard."

His mother and Johnny were watching for them as they drove up, and Marty was welcomed as a son of the family; but with Tamara and Angie it was different. Mary Thunder started out ignoring Angela in a pleasant sort of way, but by the end of the second day they were on an easy footing. Angela was helping around the house, even making bannocks under Mary's supervision, and in private Andy's mother told him that she was "quite pretty for a white girl."

As far as Tamara was concerned, Johnny adored her at first sight, and they sat around swapping stories about Chippewa Indians of Minnesota versus Chippewas of Michigan by the hour. But between his mother and Tamara, Andy could sense a wariness, like two wild creatures of the forest stalking each other, walking round and round in circles, taking each other's measure, estimating each other's strength.

Andy watched, puzzled and disturbed. How could his mother accept a white girl so easily and hold Tamara off at arm's length? Finally he said to Tamara while they were swimming the second afternoon,

"Tamara, what in heaven's name is going on with you and Mother? She and Angie are hitting it off perfectly, but you two act as though you might spring at each other's throat any minute. I don't get it."

"Don't you?" she asked, diving under a small incoming wave.

She swam under water for several yards; and when her head bobbed to the surface again, she called across to him,

"I do."

She was off again, eluding his pursuit, and she beat him to the raft and climbed onto it. Andy dragged her into the water and dunked her thoroughly before he set her on the raft again and pulled himself up beside her.

"OK," he said. "That much for you, and now let's hear. I want to know why you and my mother are fighting."

"Fighting?" spluttered Tamara, shaking herself like a wet puppy, "Why, that's ridiculous; we've scarcely spoken two words to each other!"

"That's just it!" cried Andy in exasperation, "and I want to know why."

"I wish I could explain it to you," Tamara replied, "but being a man, I don't believe you'd understand."

"You're being infuriating!" Andy exclaimed. "Can't you be serious for just one minute? Mother invited you up here herself, and now that you're here, both of you are acting horrible to each other. If I didn't know better, I'd think she was afraid we were engaged or something and was sizing you up."

There was a smile in Tamara's eyes and a quizzical little quirk at the corners of her mouth. "And vice versa, I might add," she said softly. "Here come Angie and Marty. Let's call it off."

She gave Andy a shove off the side of the raft and dived in herself.

The third day of their visit, with the situation still tense, Johnny brought in a beaver he had caught. Andy's mother turned abruptly to Tamara and said,

"How about skinning the beaver for me, Tamara, and I'll cook it for supper."

There was a long silence while Tamara looked at the dead beaver; a great play of emotion moving across her face. She turned to Andy for help, but he said nothing. Her glance swung to Johnny, but his face was perfectly passive. Finally she said, with unconcealed distress,

"Mrs. Thunder, I'm sorry, but I've never skinned a beaver

143

in my life. I don't know how."

Mary Thunder looked incredulously at her, and then, her eyes never leaving Tamara's face, she flung out these words to Andy,

"Andy, what in hell kind of a squaw is this who can't skin a beaver?"

She would never have thought of saying such a thing about a white girl, but this was an Indian, one of their own, and she could say what came into her mind. It was right, the tightness inside of Andy let go. But his mother could see that her words had cut deeper than she thought; Tamara was close to tears. Mary Thunder smiled one of her magnificent, healing smiles and said,

"Andy, it's a lovely day. Take Tamara out in *Josie's Coat* while I skin the beaver."

Then to everyone's amazement Tamara said, "No, we'll go for a boat ride *after* the beaver is skinned. I'd better watch."

She smiled her own warm smile back at Andy's mother, and the stalking period was over.

Later, just as Andy was about to take Tamara out in *Josie's Coat,* Johnny returned from a quick trip to the boatyard. Instead of stopping where he usually did, he drove down to the dock, jumped out of his old car and opened the trunk.

"Come give me a hand, Andy," he called, and stood back to let Andy and Tamara look into the trunk.

There was a ten-horse motor, scratched and battered, obviously an old model, but shining clean and polished. Andy stared at it in disbelief.

"For *Josie,*" Johnny said proudly. "I got it all fixed up. Pull her out, Andy, and let's see how she works."

"How did you get hold of this?" Andy demanded, lifting it out and starting for the boat. "It's a good motor; I know because I've worked on 'em summers."

"They was clearin' out some old stuff a couple of weeks back," said Johnny, "and they said for me to throw it on the junk pile. I looked it over and asked if I could have it and fix it up for you, and they said, 'Sure.' So I did."

"But fixing it so it'll work must have cost you quite a bit," Andy protested.

"Naw, it's old but it was in pretty good shape—just looked bad. After I got it cleaned up and put in a couple of missing parts out of the used-parts box, she ran like a top. All it cost was a couple of gallons of gas and a little of my time after hours, and I got lots of that!" He grinned and helped Andy mount the motor on *Josie*.

Andy pulled the rope, the ancient motor caught and settled into a steady hum. He gave Tamara a hand into the boat and motioned to Johnny to get in, too; but he shook his head and shouted over the noise of the motor,

"You go out alone this time. I'll have lots of chances to ride. Why don't you take Tamara to see the tower? It'll be gone next time you come. They're tearing it down."

Andy shifted into gear and headed *Josie* toward the tower. Tamara was gazing out over the water with a faraway look in her eyes. Suddenly she said,

"Andy, do you suppose I could ever be the kind of squaw your mother would like me to be? There are so many things about Indians that I don't know."

Andy was a little nonplussed at the question, but then he said,

"Tamara, you took that beaver-skinning like a veteran. You'll be just Mother's kind of squaw some day. How did you like being called a squaw anyhow?"

Tamara giggled. "Nobody ever called me that before, but you know, from her I kind of liked it!"

nineteen

"Andy's Tower" was what all his friends called the apartment Andy found just before the University opened in the fall of his sophomore year. It was three flights up in a tall Victorian house a few blocks from the place where Tamara was going to live. The steep circular stairs that led to it wound up through a dark tower and finally came out into a little round room, encircled by curving windows and a window seat. From there you walked a few steps down into the room where Andy would live.

The old man who owned the house told him no one had lived up there for two years. Andy believed it; the place was a mess: dirty floors, dust an inch thick everywhere, plaster and paint peeling from walls and ceiling, and all of it full of the stuffy smell of long-closed rooms. Tamara and Angie came to see it the minute they got into town.

"Why hasn't anybody lived up here all this time?" cried Tamara. "I think it's adorable—just like in a book!"

"You can see the whole campus from here!" Angie exclaimed. "Just look!"

She went from window to window and finally came to rest beside Tamara on the window seat. "I agree with you," she said. "It's quaint and charming, and how about those winding stairs! I should think this would be the most desirable place in the house. Why *hasn't* it been rented?"

"I can think of one awfully good reason," Andy answered. "There isn't any bathroom up here. But I guess it shouldn't bother me too much. Going down to the second floor'll be a lot easier than going to the little house out back. After my years of training, I'm the ideal tenant for this place!"

The girls came back the next day with mops, pails, scrub brushes and rags. Andy had persuaded his landlord to pay for paint and something to patch the plaster with, and he, himself, would do the work. They'd talked about his rent, too. If he would agree to do the chores around the place, like mowing the lawn, shoveling snow and raking leaves, he would be credited with a third of his rent. That was great for Andy, because in spite of his various student-aid funds, all his economies and savings from summer work, he was always short of money.

"My landlord's a million years old and kind of shaky," he told the girls. "He needs help and I need dough."

Marty and Mike came over and helped him patch plaster, and then they all worked at painting the walls. After they dried, the girls hung splashy psychedelic posters on them and stood back to admire their work.

"It's cool," Tamara decided, "but it's sure far out!"

"No farther out than *Josie's Coat*," said Angie, laughing.

"True," Andy nodded. "Kind of makes me think of the old girl. Guess that's why I like it."

Each of the walls was painted a different color: red, orange, green and white, and the effect was dazzling to say the least. But it was clean and fresh and cheerful; the musty smell of old houses was gone. Next they turned critical eyes on the furniture.

"It's horrible," was Angie's judgment. "You'll break your back if you sleep on that studio couch, Andy. It's full of hummocks."

"Well, I'll just have to make do with what's here," said Andy firmly. "I haven't any money for furniture."

Tamara had been rummaging around in the attic that opened off his room and came back dragging a heavy old oak table, good and sturdy except for one crippled leg.

"It's a lot better for you to study on than that crummy old desk," she commented. "Somebody can mend this leg, and I'll paint it."

Mike put a screw or two in the leg, and Tamara began slapping green paint on it. Angela was still moaning over the battered studio couch. Suddenly she cried,

"Take that thing to the attic, Andy. I need you and the VW, Marty. Come on."

She raced through the attic and down the back stairs with Marty following. Andy, Tamara and Mike, left behind, looked at each other, shrugged their shoulders and went back to work. Tamara and Andy cleaned the filthy stove and sink while Mike tackled the refrigerator. Then they went out to buy some groceries, and Andy made coffee and started spaghetti for supper.

"The first meal in Andy's Tower," he said. "Won't Angie and Marty be surprised? Wonder when they'll be back."

149

"Heaven knows," Mike said. "They could have gone anywhere. Let's eat as soon as the spaghetti's done. I'm starved."

Tamara and Andy washed the heterogeneous collection of dishes and set the table. Just as the meal was ready and they were sitting down to eat, they heard calls for help from the back stairs. Angie and Marty were back from their trip, with the VW bus jammed to the roof. A hide-a-bed took up the most room, but there were two elderly uphostered chairs, a rolled-up rug, some old cushions and miscellaneous packages.

Angie refused to answer any questions until everything was lugged upstairs and Andy had dished up more spaghetti and poured hot coffee all around.

Then she explained, "While I was sputtering about that old studio couch today, I suddenly remembered a remark of my mother's just before I left to come back to school. She'd been having our rec room repainted, new curtains and stuff, and she said she must remember to call the Salvation Army or Good Will to come and get the old hide-a-bed. So I called her from the phone booth on the corner and she still had it plus some other things she'd decided to replace. She said to come right out and see what we could use in Andy's Tower. So we went out to Stillwater, and here it is."

"Those cushions will be dandy on the window seat in the Tower," Tamara assured her.

"Yeah, that's what I thought." Angie nodded. "So I took 'em and Mother hunted until she found some material she bought at a sale once and never had any place to use. Here it is in this sack. She thought we could make new covers."

"Let's do it right now!" Tamara exclaimed. "That's the most gorgeous red."

Everybody helped with the dishes, then the boys washed the dirty windows and laid Mrs. Chester's old beige rug on the floor while the girls stitched up the cushion covers by hand.

"What a miracle everything goes with the paint so well! I *love* it," purred Tamara, looking at the soft green hide-a-bed, beige-print chairs and red cushions. "I wish I lived here. My room is going to seem awfully stodgy compared to this!"

"I know," Angela sighed. "The sorority house is so blah, but I have to live there because my mother did when she was at the U. I wish we could fix a place like this for us, Tammy."

"Well, I've got to admit the place has lots of personality," said Marty, looking around the renovated room. "Your mom's timing was perfect, Angie. The old furniture has done wonders. What would you call this decor?"

Angela giggled. "Neo-Victorian garret," she responded, "and I love it!"

Evidently all of Andy's friends loved it, because the whole fall term they kept climbing the circular stairs to see it and staying to drink coffee and talk about a dozen different things. Andy hadn't known he *had* so many friends; they especially liked sitting on the window seat in the Tower, looking out over the campus and the city. Quite often Andy worked at the library in the evenings, but that didn't seem to deter people from dropping in. He'd find them there even when he came home late and tired, planning to crawl right into bed. So he devised a plan to limit the whole thing just a bit. First, he began locking the Tower door when he went out. Then he told everybody that he wasn't having "open house" unless the Tower light was on. When he wanted to study at home, he kept the Tower dark and had a light only in the main room. After a few false starts, with people forgetting and coming up anyway, it worked very well, and no one seemed to get mad about it.

Before Andy knew it, cold weather had come and Thanksgiving was there. They had just one day off for the holiday, so nobody but Angela could have Thanksgiving dinner at home. Her mother invited Andy, Tamara and Marty to come for the day, and they all went.

When they got back to the U. that evening, full and content, they found Fred Beaudoin sitting on Andy's steps in the cold, waiting for them.

"Your landlord told me you'd be back tonight, Andy," he greeted them. "I thought I'd wait."

"Sure enough," Andy said cordially. "Come on up and get warm, Fred."

They went into the hall, and Andy unlocked the door. All of them groped their way up the steep steps to the Tower room, and Andy fumbled for the chain that turned on the light, wondering what had brought Fred over. It must be something crucial if it couldn't wait until morning. He blinked in the sudden light and turned to Fred.

"Your mother isn't sick, is she?" he demanded, anxiously.

"Nope, Ma's feelin' swell, just swell, thanks!" Fred beamed, rubbing his hands.

Andy sniffed suspiciously. "You aren't drinking again, Fred?"

"Nope, I ain't had nothing to drink since you took me over to the Club," he said firmly.

He sat down on the hide-a-bed and stared expectantly at Andy, waiting for his next question, grinning widely all the time.

"Well," said Andy, sitting down beside him, "let's have it. What's up?"

The others were watching them, waiting to hear, too. Fred looked around the circle and then back at Andy.

"Ma and me had the best Thanksgivin' Day we ever had," he said finally.

"We're glad to hear that," Andy said politely. "Were you invited out?"

"Nope, we had it to home," he answered. "A friend give us a turkey, and Ma cooked it in our own stove."

Andy remembered the two-burner gas plate in their forlorn room and waited for Fred to go on.

"I got me a job yesterday, folks. Or probably I oughta say Mr. LeMon got it for me. A feller come to see him who wanted a caretaker for a fourplex he owns over near the West Bank. Been havin' a lotta trouble lately with it bein' broke into so he wanted somebody to live on the place. Said there was a little apartment in the basement a person could live in."

As he listened to Fred, Andy was watching Tamara's face. He could see that she was about to burst with excitement. Any second he expected her to break in and finish the story herself, taking all the wind out of poor Fred's sails. He caught her eye and put his finger on his lips, shaking his head at her. She nodded, and Andy said,

153

"Great, Fred! What happened?"

"Well," Fred went on, "I was in the office when the man come in, and he said to Mr. LeMon that he always sent him such good men to work for him, did he have one now? Him and his wife are leavin' for a couple of months in Florida next week, and he wanted to get a man right away and get him settled."

Fred stopped for a moment and looked slowly around the group again,

"You could never guess in a million years what Mr. LeMon said. He looked right at that man and said, 'Mr. Beaudoin here is exactly the man you're looking for, and he's in the market for a job. You can count on him.' He called me *Mr. Beaudoin,* and he said he could count on *me!*"

Andy cleared his throat and said, "Did you accept the job?"

"Did I *what?*" Fred shouted. "D'you think I'm crazy, man? When he asked when could I come, I said, 'Today if you want. Only one question, can my ma and her cat come live there, too?' He said sure thing she could. It would be nice for the ladies in the fourplex to have a woman helping around the place."

Tamara couldn't contain herself any longer. "So you moved, and you had Thanksgiving there!"

Fred smiled at her. 'Yeah, we moved, all right. Mr. LeMon took me in his car, and we got Ma, the cat, our clothes and a few keepsakes Ma wanted to save, and we just walked outta that place and went right to the new apartment. It didn't take more'n an hour."

"Is there a bedroom for your mother?" Andy asked, holding his breath.

"A bedroom for Ma," he nodded. "And a nice livin' room with a hide-a-what d'you call it? Anyhow it's like this one I'm settin' on, for me to sleep on, and a kitchen with a real stove with an oven, so Ma could roast the turkey, and a bathroom with a tub and *lots* of hot water. And *clean!* Ma says she ain't never lived in such a clean place since she left home, and it's all furnished—real nice stuff, too."

Marty spoke up for the first time. "Is the man going to pay you anything for taking care of the place, or do you just get a place to live?" he asked practically.

"Oh sure, he's going to pay me," Fred said. "It ain't goin' to be a lot, but it'll buy us enough to eat, with some left over, and Ma's got her old age pension, you know. We'll make do just fine."

He got up to go. "Best be on my way," he said, "but I had to tell you folks about our good luck. What a Thanksgiving! Ma said I was to ask you to come see our new home soon as you can."

He included them all in his words, but his eyes were on Andy's face.

"I have to be getting back to the house, too," Marty said, putting on his jacket. "I'll run you home, Fred."

"Me too?" inquired Angie.

"You too," he said, "and Tamara."

"You're all leaving at once," complained Andy. "You stay awhile, and I'll walk you home, Tamara."

"OK," she agreed, "but not long. I've got a psych. quiz tomorrow."

They watched the others go down the winding stair, and then Andy said,

155

"In spite of that enormous dinner, I'm starving, Tamara."

Tamara laughed. "So am I," she said, "although when we got through eating, I thought I could never eat again."

Andy went to the cupboard and looked over the cans of soup. "What do you want, split pea or bean and bacon?"

"Bean and bacon," she decided.

It was soon hot, and they sat side by side on the hide-a-bed with their soup and the box of crackers between them.

"I'll never forget Fred's face when he said, 'What a Thanksgiving!'" Tamara said, blowing on her soup.

"Yeah, it was something to see, wasn't it?" Andy agreed. "Nice that you were all here."

"Well, yes; it was nice for us, but it was plain that Fred came to tell *you*, Andy. He knows that he owes everything to you. If it hadn't been for you insisting that something could be done for him, and going right ahead, when everybody else, even his own mother, doubted, he'd probably have spent Thanksgiving at the Workhouse again."

"Nonsense!" said Andy, "It wasn't all me. Wow, that soup is hot!" He stuck out his tongue and waved it around to cool it.

Tamara giggled, but went back to her conversation. "Well, who found out about the Indian Neighborhood Club and got him started and stuck by him?"

"You can't ever give up on people, I guess," Andy answered thoughtfully. "What if Bob had given up on me? Where would I be now?"

"I don't know," Tamara smiled, "but I'm glad you're here. You *are* going into the School of Social Work next fall, aren't you?"

"What makes you think I should be a social worker?" Andy parried. "Bob and Ann, especially, think I'm cut out to be a teacher."

"Fred Beaudoin makes me think you should be a social worker, Andy Thunder," Tamara told him. "Bob and Ann haven't seen you here in the city. They just don't know."

"Well, it takes more than one swallow to make a summer, my grandmother always used to say." Andy yawned. "There's still lots of time to decide. Come on, Tamara. Time for you to go home."

twenty

Andy went home for Christmas; Tamara wanted him to go to Michigan with her for at least part of the holidays, but he couldn't afford it.

"I'm just barely going to make it this year as it is, without any extra expenses," he said ruefully. "Maybe I can come over next summer, Tamara. I'd like to meet your folks."

Although he didn't mention it, Andy had another reason for wanting a long holiday at home. He needed to talk to Bob about his major, which had to be settled before the spring term was over, and he was still undecided. On the long bus ride home he had plenty of time to think about it without interruption, but he still hadn't come to any decision when Bob came out to the village a day or so after Christmas and took Andy back to town with him.

"Ann says she's hardly had a glimpse of you since you came home, so she sent me for you. You're to stay for dinner and get acquainted with Andrea," Bob said. Andrea was the baby girl born just a week after Andy went back to the U. in the fall.

Ann met them at the door and put the baby into Andy's arms.

"If she'd been a boy, we were going to name her after you," she said, "but our Andrew turned into Andrea, the best we could do for you."

Andy held her as if she were a bit of fragile china.

"My goodness," said Ann, helping him out of his jacket, "you don't need to be afraid of her; she won't break. Babies are remarkably tough!"

"But she's so tiny," said Andy, in a voice scarcely above a whisper.

He tiptoed gingerly to a chair and sat down. "What shall I do with her?" he asked. "Does she like to lie down or sit up, or what?"

He laid her across his lap, and she began to fuss.

"There, see!" he exclaimed. "I've done something wrong. She's going to cry. You take her."

"No, you keep her," Ann urged. "She's your namesake, and besides, I want to get some coffee. She likes to sit up, but you have to support her back; she can't sit alone yet."

She set the baby up, arranged her against his arm, and went into the kitchen. Bob came into the room and smiled at the two of them. But when she started to cry again, he took her.

Andy gave a relieved sigh. "Gee, you do it so easy," he said admiringly. "I'm scared of 'em. She's awfully cute, though."

"All it takes is a little practice," Bob assured him, balancing Andrea expertly on his knee. "You'll learn someday."

"Not for a long time," Andy said, grinning. "I've got a long way to go before I have one of those. I have a lot of decisions to make before I decide to get married."

So that evening after the children were tucked into bed, they sat down to discuss Andy's first decision, his major at the University. The talk went on far into the night, and was continued for several more nights during vacation. Sometimes at the Underhills', sometimes at home.

For Ann there was no question as to the right decision. Bob was a teacher; she had been a teacher before Bobby was born, and planned to return when the children were old enough. Andy was cut out to be a teacher, too, and should put all thought of social work as a career out of his mind.

Andy's mother thought there was such great need for Indian social workers in the city that perhaps Andy should go into the School of Social Work, as Tamara wanted.

"I think maybe it's easier to get good teachers than good social workers for our people," she said hesitantly. "What do you think, Johnny?"

Johnny didn't care too much what Andy decided as long as he stayed in school and graduated.

It was the night before Andy was to go back for the winter term. They were all sitting around the wood stove at the Thunders', after eating one of Mary's great Indian suppers.

"I've got to know what I'm going to do before I leave here tomorrow morning," Andy said firmly. "I'm sick and tired of putting it off, leaving a lot of loose ends hanging out in my life."

"Maybe you should wait and let Tamara help you decide," his mother suggested.

"No," Andy protested. "Tamara really doesn't have anything to say about this, and anyhow, we've talked about it a

lot and I know exactly what she thinks. I'm not tied to
Tamara and what she wants. The way you talk you'd think
we were engaged."

He looked around the group and caught the quick little
smile that passed between his mother and Ann. It was gone
in an instant, and the two women sat and stared primly at
him.

"She is very beautiful," said his mother, softly.

"And very smart," Ann took up the litany.

"And *I* think she would make you a very good wife," finished Johnny.

"Oh, good Lord!" moaned Andy. "We aren't going to decide whether Tamara would make me a good wife or not!
How did we get into this, anyhow?"

And then Bob, who had been saying nothing, stepped into
the breach.

"I agree that Tamara is a honey, but let's leave her strictly
out of this discussion. Some other day he'll probably have to
decide about her, but when that day comes, none of us will
be invited to sit in council with him! Right, Andy?"

"Right!" Andy nodded.

"OK," said Bob. "Now let's try to get the whole thing together. As I see it, he needs to answer just two questions very
honestly. Here's number one, Andy.

"Do you really want to be a social worker?"

Silence fell on the little room; there was no sound but the
crackling of the fire in the stove. Finally Andy answered.

"No, I don't think so. I like doing what I did for the Beaudoins, but I'm sure I wouldn't have to be a career social
worker to do those things for people."

"All right," agreed Bob. "Question number two: Do you really want to be a teacher? Now, this one may be harder to be honest about. You have to ask yourself whether or not you are being influenced by us. Take your time."

Andy was deliberate, but when he answered, there was no uncertainty in his voice. He looked straight at Bob and said clearly,

"Yes, I am sure I want to be a teacher, either history or perhaps English. Now don't faint, Ann! I've hesitated a long time making up my mind; I've thought a lot about it and talked to people at the U. Most of my friends at school, including Tamara, of course, have tried to push me the other way, but after all, shouldn't a man have a chance to do what he *wants* to do?"

"Hurray, well-spoken!" cried Ann, "You'll graduate from the College of Ed. and then you'll come back home to teach. You'll come back to our school, won't you?"

"Ann, you be quiet," warned Bob. "You're just confusing the issue."

Andy stood up and stretched. "I've decided the first part, and I'm glad," he said. "But don't anybody try to rush me about what comes next. Maybe it will be even longer than two years before I meet up with that."

"Why?" demanded his mother.

"Well, I'm thinking of dropping out of the U. next year and working awhile before I finish my degree," Andy answered casually, avoiding her eyes.

There, he'd dropped the bomb! He walked to the window and looked out at the dark, frozen lake. Johnny finally broke the stunned silence.

"But *gwe-we-zance*," he protested, reverting to his old name for Andy, "why should you drop out now? You been doing so good."

"Your marks are wonderful," his mother said, "and I've heard that if an Indian gets through the first two years of college, he's got it made. Isn't that so, Bob?"

"That may be so," Andy broke in before Bob could answer, "but I've also heard that most Indian kids have to drop out, sometimes even more than once, to earn their way through. I've been lucky so far, but I've got the feeling that my luck is about to run out."

"Why, Andy?" Bob said quietly.

"Well," Andy began, "I found out the other day that a couple of my loans run out at the end of two years, and they aren't renewable. Neither one is terribly big, but added together they've been keeping me in school. If I don't have them, there won't be enough money to pay my rent. Or if I pay the rent, then I won't be able to pay my tuition. Or if I pay the tuition, I couldn't buy any books. You can't imagine how high books are these days. It's just as simple as that."

He spread his hands out, palms up, and grinned. Then he saw the hurt, disturbed look on his mother's face and sobered quickly.

"Mom, please! It isn't any big deal. It happens all the time to lots of students: white, black, red, yellow. Kids are forever dropping in and out of the U. It may not even happen. I'm going to see if I can land a better paying job next year, or maybe another loan will come my way, who knows? Lots of things can happen between now and next fall. Probably I shouldn't even have mentioned it tonight, but I thought maybe it would be better to warn you that it *might* happen, and then you wouldn't be as upset as if it hit you cold, see?"

Bob nodded approvingly. "I think you're right. I had to drop out for a couple of terms and my family nearly died. But it worked out all right."

"I think your mother is afraid you might not go back to finish if you drop out next year," Ann suggested.

Mary Thunder nodded. "Exactly," she said. "It's so easy to get out of the habit of studying and into the habit of earning regular money. I'd hate for that to happen with you, Andrew."

Andy smiled at her reassuringly. "Don't worry, Mom," he said. "It won't. Too many people would be on my back, including Tamara."

Johnny had been staring thoughtfully at Andy and now he spoke. "My boss has offered me a year 'round job at the boatyard, Andy," he said. "We get snowmobiles to work on now in the winter. Starting next fall I can send you money every payday. You stay right there in school, and we'll manage. There will be money."

"No, Johnny!" Andy exclaimed when he could speak. "You kept me in high school three years. You need every cent of the money you earn to live on. You know how much I thank you, but no! I won't have it!"

twenty-one

Andy made his peace with Tamara; she wasn't too bothered about his deciding to teach, as long as he stayed in the Twin Cities to do it. But he wouldn't promise that, so during the rest of that year he sometimes caught her looking at him with an unhappy, brooding expression in her eyes.

In a letter that he wrote to his mother near the end of the spring term, Andy warned her again not to be shocked if he turned up in June with all his possessions, ready to be her permanent boarder for the next year. He had been investigating jobs and student loans and none of them seemed to offer him enough help. He really thought the only way out was a year of work and saving.

"If I get a halfway decent job and scrimp enough, I ought to be able to make it the rest of the way through," he told her.

A letter came back by return mail. "Be at home Saturday afternoon," his mother wrote tersely. "Johnny is bringing me down to visit."

Andy was shocked speechless. This would be the first time she had come to see him on campus. At various times she had gone to see his older brothers and sisters when they were away at school, but those schools were in smaller towns. The very thought of the big city seemed to frighten her, so he had never urged her to come. Her letter arrived on Monday. Tamara, Angie and Marty came over that evening so he read it to them.

"We'll have a dinner!" the girls cried.

"They'll be spending the night," said Marty, practically. "We'll have to arrange a place for them to stay."

"We have the guest room at the Pi Phi house, you know," Angie reminded them, "and I can see if anybody's signed up for it this weekend. I'd love to have your mother stay there, Andy."

"That would be nice," Tamara interposed hesitantly, "but I know my roommate is going to be away over the weekend, and I wonder if Andy's mother might not be more comfortable with me."

"I don't see why," Angie began, and then she realized what Tamara had in mind. "Oh, I see what you mean," she said. "OK, maybe she would like it better."

"How about breakfast Sunday morning, Angie?" Tamara asked. "Do you 'spose we could come over to the Pi Phi house for that?"

"Of course," Angie nodded.

"Thanks a lot," Andy said gratefully. "Johnny can stay with me, but I can't imagine what I'd do with my mother."

"Good!" agreed Marty. "My part will be to take them sightseeing in the VW Sunday morning, and then we'll have to think of a place they'd enjoy going for dinner. We'll all go—my treat."

"Oh no!" Andy exclaimed. "That's too much."

"Listen," Marty insisted, "your mother has cooked all those great meals for me up at Vermilion. Now this is my chance to take her out for dinner. You know I'm crazy about Mary Thunder! If I were a little older, and she were a little younger, Johnny wouldn't have a look-in!" He grinned at Angie, and she made a face at him.

That was Monday evening. Tuesday night Andy was working on a term paper with the Tower dark and the door locked when he heard a frantic pounding and Angie's voice screaming his name over and over. He rushed down, and she fell into his arms, sobbing hysterically.

"What's wrong?" he demanded. "What's happened?"

And as she continued to sob he shook her sharply. "Angie, stop it—tell me what's the matter."

Angie gulped down her sobs enough to wail, "Tamara's in the hospital. Oh, it was so terrible! I still can't imagine how it could have happened."

Andy felt as though an icy hand were closing off his breath. They ran out to Angie's car. "You drive, Andy," she said. "I don't think I can. Go to University Hospital. I took her there."

Then she began to tell him, shakily, what had happened. Tamara had heard that Mrs. Beaudoin was ill, so they had decided to take her some food. Tamara made her custard, Angie bought some fruit, and they set out in the car. It was almost dark when they parked in front of the fourplex. Angie took her fruit and started toward the building while

Tamara was lifting the dish of custard carefully out of the back seat. All of a sudden Angie heard Tamara scream, and spun around just in time to see a man plunge out of the shadows and grab her.

The dish of custard flew out of her hands and crashed on the sidewalk as Tamara began to claw and kick at the man. Angie's one thought was to get to Fred for help. She rushed into the building, shrieking his name, and he came running out of the apartment. Angie babbled something about a man and Tamara; so Fred ran back, grabbed his mother's cane and raced out the door. Tamara was still struggling and screaming, and the man was dragging her along the sidewalk by her hair.

"If she hadn't put up such a fight," Angie said, "he would have disappeared with her by the time we got back. Fred shouted and whacked at him with his mother's cane. Then the beast dropped Tamara and swung on Fred, but Fred kept right on yelling and beating him with the cane, and suddenly the man ran across the street and just vanished."

"Where did he go?" Andy demanded. "Wasn't there anybody around to stop him?"

"Well," Angie answered uncertainly, "I can't seem to remember about that. The neighbors all came running out, and somebody went to call the police."

Angie had knelt down beside Tamara where she lay only half-conscious on the sidewalk, moaning over and over, "Get Andy, get Andy." Fred came and said the police would soon be there, but Tamara kept begging for Andy. So finally, under cover of the commotion, Fred had picked her up and laid her in the back seat of Angie's car, and he and Angie had started for University Hospital with her.

"I know it was against all the rules to move her," Angie confessed, "but I couldn't bear to let her lie there on that dirty sidewalk, all bleeding and everything. The police won't do anything to me, will they?"

"I don't think so," Andy answered. "They'll probably be glad that you moved quick enough to keep her from being raped—you and Fred, too."

"Well, I hope so," Angie was half sobbing again. "All I could think of was to get her to the hospital. She was in the emergency room when I left. The nurses were washing off the blood so the doctor could tell how bad she was hurt, and she still kept pleading for you."

Andy was trying desperately to stay calm for Angie's sake, but he was trembling inside.

"Did he say how bad he thought it was?" Andy asked as quietly as possible.

"No, he had just begun to examine her," Angie said. "I heard him say to the nurse that she was in shock."

Andy stepped harder on the accelerator, and the Toyota leaped forward.

"I'm ashamed that I acted like such a baby when I got to the Tower," Angie apologized. "I was quite proud of myself, thinking how strong I was, until I went and caved in!"

"Don't even think about it," Andy tried to soothe her. "You were just getting the reaction, the way anybody would."

"But what if Fred hadn't been home?" she cried, living the scene over again, and Andy decided it would be best to let her talk about it. "There wasn't a minute to spare, Andy. That man was like a wild beast. He leaped on her like a tiger. There wasn't anyone in sight when I got out of the car." She shuddered.

They were at the hospital now. Andy fortunately found a parking place right away, and he and Angie hurried to the emergency room. A nurse met them at the door.

"You're Andy?" she asked him, and smiled when he nodded. "She's going to be glad to see you. She's beginning to come out of shock, but she's still asking to see Andy."

All Tamara could say when he leaned over her was, "Oh Andy," very softly. She could rest now, relaxed and at ease, her eyes closed while he sat beside her, holding her hand, looking at the scrapes and scratches on her face, and her hands and arms. The doctor came in and told him that in addition to the cut on her forehead she had a rather deep gash on one leg. Angie thought she had been cut by the broken custard dish.

"Took a couple of dozen stitches to close those two cuts," the doctor said. "Besides, she's got a whole bunch of scrapes and bruises; even more of them will show up tomorrow. You'll look like a rainbow, young lady."

Then he went on talking to Andy. "She's been in shock, of course, but she's doing all right. We'd like to keep her overnight, just to make sure everything is OK."

Tamara roused at his last words. "Don't leave me, Andy. Please, *please* don't go!"

She clung to his hand and her eyes began to get the wild, frightened look again. The doctor said soothingly,

"Andy's staying right here with you as long as you need him. You don't need to be afraid anymore."

"I need him always," Tamara murmured, and closed her eyes again.

The doctor patted them both on the shoulder and left, giving orders for her to be moved into another room for the night. As they were taking her down the hall, a police officer came to check on her and to report that a man had been caught hiding in a backyard nearby. They suspected he was the one who had attacked her, but he needed a few more details from Tamara.

"Not tonight," said the nurse firmly, brushing past him and whisking Tamara out of sight through a door.

Angie, calm and poised by that time, stepped forward and told him that she had witnessed the whole affair and probably could tell him more, actually, than Tamara could. Wouldn't that do? He said he guessed it would be all right. Fred looked in on Tamara and Andy and whispered that if he wasn't needed any longer he'd go home and take care of Ma. Andy tried to thank him for what he had done, and Fred went home, beaming.

A few minutes later Angie came and whispered that she'd gotten rid of the policeman for the time being and she wanted to go and talk to Marty. He didn't know what had happened yet. Tamara roused enough to say dreamily,

"Goodnight, Angie. I love you." Then she drifted off again, clutching Andy's hand.

A nurse came in around midnight with a cup of hot coffee for him. She looked at Tamara and said softly to Andy,

"She's sleeping soundly. Why don't you step out in the hall for awhile and stretch your legs?"

"I don't think I'd better try," Andy said. "Her grip on my hand relaxes when she's sleeping, but every time I try to move, she grabs tighter again."

"I can't say that I blame her," said the nurse.

She went out noiselessly, and the night wore on. Andy couldn't remember ever staying awake all night before, not even the time he got locked in the old tower on the lake. But for some reason it didn't seem long or hard to stay awake. Perhaps he may have slept for a few minutes just before dawn, because suddenly he felt Tamara's hand stir in his, and when he opened his eyes and looked at her, she was wide awake.

"You did stay," she said softly. "I wondered if you'd be here when I woke up. You didn't leave me for a minute, did you?"

"Of course I didn't leave you," Andy murmured, "and I'm never going to leave you again as long as we live, Tamara; that's the way I want it to be with us. Do you?"

"Forever and forever, that's the way I want it to be, too," she whispered.

She sat up, serene and beautiful, held out her arms, and he gathered her to him.

After breakfast the doctor came in, looked at her cuts and scrapes, and said Andy had been good medicine for her. She could go home if she would promise to take life easy for a few days and not walk much until the cut on her leg had had a chance to heal. While Tamara was dressing, Andy called Marty and he came over with the bus to pick them up. A nurse arrived with a wheelchair, but Andy grinned at her, picked Tamara up in his arms and carried her out into the sunshine where Angie was waiting, looking somewhat pale and drawn after the ordeal of the night.

She took one good look at Tamara and exclaimed, "Good heavens, what's happened to you? You look positively radiant. I expected to see you looking wan this morning, to say the least. I look like an old hag!"

Tamara laughed and looked questioningly at Andy. He nodded, so she said,

"Well, Andy sat beside me all night and this morning he asked me to marry him."

"Ho, ho!" exclaimed Marty. "I'd be tempted to try it on Angie if I thought it would work. She sure looks peaked this morning."

They all laughed.

"We'll have an engagement party when Andy's mother and Johnny come," Angie said. "Won't they be surprised!"

"I hardly think so," Andy responded. "They've had Tamara and me engaged for at least six months."

That was Wednesday. Saturday afternoon when Johnny's hearty "Hello!" came roaring up the stairs, they were all together in Andy's Tower. Tamara was on the hide-a-bed with her leg up, Angie and Marty were cooking dinner, and Andy was dividing his attention between Tamara and the Tower windows, where he went every few minutes to look for his mother and Johnny.

When Andy ushered them into the room, the first thing they saw, of course, was Tamara on the couch still looking quite battered.

"What in the world happened to you, child!" Andy's mother exclaimed.

They left it to Angie to tell the story because she knew more about it than anyone else, and besides, she could make it more dramatic.

"And so everybody went home and left Tamara in the hospital all night with Andy to hold her hand," finished Angela, "and now Andy has to finish the story himself. He knows more about that than I do."

The room was silent; everybody looked at Andy.

"You tell them, Tamara," he urged.

Tamara shook her head. "Oh no, Andy. This is for you to tell."

"Well-l-l," Andy fumbled around for the words, and finally blurted out, "the story ended all right. I guess all I can say is, 'And they lived happily ever after,' Mom, the way the stories you used to tell us always ended!"

"You mean you and Tamara are engaged at last?" his mother cried.

She took Tamara in her arms, very gently so as not to hurt the sore places. The two pairs of black eyes smiled into each other, and Tamara said softly so only Mary Thunder could hear,

"What in hell kind of a squaw do you think I'll make for him?"

"Just the kind of squaw he needs, Tamara," Mary Thunder whispered back.

"Good heavens!" screamed Angie, "supper's burning. I forgot!"

So everyone's attention was diverted and nobody asked what the private joke was. Angie rushed to the stove to rescue the pork chops and scalloped potatoes, Andy pulled himself together enough to make the coffee, Marty set the table, and they were eating in no time. For dessert Angie brought in a big angel cake, trimmed with pink frosting rosebuds and *Tamara and Andy* across the top in green frosting script. She set it in front of Tamara and handed her a knife.

"I told you we'd have an engagement party," she said. "I didn't make the cake," she admitted, "but I decorated it myself. Help her cut it, Andy."

Johnny held up his hand. "Wait one minute before you cut it," he said, "we have some news, Mary and me. You want to tell 'em, Mary?"

Mary nodded, "Ours isn't exciting, like yours," she began, "because we're old folks, but we want you to know that Johnny and I have decided to get married, very soon—"

"Like next Saturday," Johnny interrupted. "You've all got to come."

Mary smiled at him. With his eyes intent on his mother's face, Andy saw the warm blush under the bronze of her cheeks and knew that she found it *very* exciting, in spite of her remark about "old folks."

"We decided this all of a sudden," she went on, "although we've been thinking about it for quite awhile."

"We sure have," Johnny broke in again, "something like thirty-five years!"

Mary put her finger on his lips and continued, "I wanted to wait until later in the summer so more of the children could come, but Johnny said, 'No, next Saturday!'"

Johnny took her hand and held it firmly.

"We waited long enough," he rumbled. "We should have done this a long time ago. No more waiting! My foot is put down!"

The whole room was in an uproar. Finals would begin the week after, but Marty expressed it for all of them,

"To heck with finals. I don't care if I flunk every one of 'em. I wouldn't miss seeing you two married for anything!"

"Cut the cake, Tamara. What an engagement party this turned out to be!" cried Angie.

175

It was much later, when they were about to separate for the night, that Andy remembered to ask his mother what brought them to the campus in the beginning.

"Was it the wedding you came to tell us about or was there something else, too?" he asked.

"Oh, my goodness, Andy!" his mother exclaimed. "It's so good that you thought to ask me. We might have gotten all the way back to Lake Vermilion before I remembered it again."

All of them were watching Mary as she reached into her handbag and pulled out a small black book. She handed it silently to Andy, and at his surprised look she said briefly, "Open it."

Andy obeyed and inside found the record of a savings account in his mother's name. There had been only one deposit, made in June, five years before, in the amount of $1,800.00. Interest had accumulated and there had been no withdrawals, so now Andy was staring in utter bewilderment at a staggering balance of well over $2,000.00. Suddenly he understood what he was seeing.

"No, no, Mom," he cried. "It's not mine! I told you it was yours to use for something you wanted for yourself. I won't take it, Mom."

"You will take it, Andrew," his mother answered him firmly. "I put it away for you to have someday when you needed it. I think this is the time."

"But Mom." Andy protested, "you've spoiled all my plans for it. I *wondered* what had become of that money, but I never had the nerve to ask you. You never spent a penny of it for yourself."

"I did, too," his mother said. "I bought myself a pretty summer dress. It's been my best one ever since; you must remember that dress. It was the first brand new one I'd had in years and years."

Mother and son were talking to each other now as though they were all alone in the room.

"But it wasn't just for a dress, Mom," Andy said sternly. "It was for something big. I wanted you to have running water in the house or something important like that. I should have checked into it sooner. I should have insisted that you use it for yourself."

"Andy," his mother said softly, "I don't think you understand at all. I am doing exactly what you told me to do with that money. I *am* using it for something I want for myself very, very much. I guess I want it more than anything else in the world right now; I s'pose I'm really being selfish. I want you to finish school without a break. You don't seem to understand how important that is to me."

Andy made one last attempt. "But now that you and Johnny are going to be married, you need so many things for yourself, for the house."

His voice trailed off uncertainly, for Johnny had risen and was standing in front of him.

"Let your mama have her way, *gwe-we-zance,*" he said. "Let her use this money you gave her for what *she* wants. I told you I'm going to be working all-year 'round now. I will give her whatever she needs."

Andy looked from his mother to Johnny, and then back at his mother again. He nodded, and then smiled. Suddenly he understood Johnny perfectly.

twenty-two

The land was aglow with spring when Andy and his friends drove up to Lake Vermilion the next Saturday for the wedding. Tamara sat beside Andy in Marty's VW bus, looking as beautiful as the spring day, he thought, even though her face was still marred by scratches and bruises. She had scooped up her long black hair and twisted it into a big, soft knot like a crown on the top of her head. And she was wearing a dress he had never seen before, white and billowy and printed all over with spring flowers.

"I have to look as nice as possible with this battered face, if I'm to be your mother's bridesmaid," she told Andy.

When they arrived, the people of the village were all streaming down the hill and gathering on the grass in front of the house. The Underhills had come with Bobby and Andrea. The Major's boat was just easing up to the dock. Mary Thunder, in a new pink dress with white flowers that Johnny had given her pinned to the shoulder, was walking among her guests, smiling and cordial as she welcomed each one. It came to Andy then, as he watched her, that his mother would always have her own quiet dignity, no matter where she might be placed.

The minister and his wife were the last to come, and soon afterward he stood in front of the people with Mary and Johnny facing him, Tamara and Andy beside them.

"Dearly beloved," he began, "we are gathered together to join this man and this woman in holy matrimony. . . ."

John and Mary repeated their vows, to each other, as though they were all alone on the green hillside. Andy found it hard to keep his mind on the ceremony; his thoughts kept drifting back to the people who must have made their vows perhaps on that very hillside, his own people, in the musical tongue of the Ojibway, or perhaps with no words at all.

Afterward he vaguely remembered pulling the ring out of his pocket to give to the minister at the right time, and he noticed that Tamara gave the ring to him also at the proper moment, and then the minister was saying,

"I now pronounce you man and wife. Whom God hath joined together, let no man put asunder."

The wedding guests surged around Mary and Johnny to wish them well, and Tamara, all smiles and tears ran to Andy.

"I wish *we* were getting married this afternoon, Andy," she whispered. "We couldn't, could we?"

Andy looked down at her, about to laugh, but he noticed just in time that the smile was gone from her face. He took her hand and drew her away from the crowd. They walked down to the edge of the lake and he helped her into *Josie's*

Coat and stepped in beside her.

"Let's sit here for awhile, Tamara, you're tired. And besides, I want to know what brought on that question."

To answer him she repeated the question, "We couldn't get married this afternoon, could we? Why couldn't the minister just go ahead and marry us, too?"

"Well," replied Andy gravely, "I can think of two very good reasons. In the first place, you have to have a thing called a license to get married. I know it seems silly, but the state says you must, so that's all there is to it."

"Pooh!" said Tamara, making a face, "I think that's very un-Indian."

"Oh, I agree," nodded Andy, "but there's another reason; we have two more years of school, or have you forgotten? And we have no money."

"Money? Who needs money?" Tamara inquired. "It's the two years that really worry me. Two years is such a long time. So many things can go wrong in two years."

Andy tried to tease her out of her dark mood. "You just try to lose me and see what happens to you, Tamara Jay," he warned her.

"I know," brooded Tamara, "I feel that way, too, you can't ever lose me, but still I just have this bad feeling. I have the feeling that if we don't get married right away, we might not get married at all. Lots of students get married while they're in school. Why can't we?"

They sat in silence a few minutes watching the people milling about on the hillside, waiting to be served coffee, fruit punch and cookies. Finally Andy answered her.

"I don't like to be engaged so long, either, Tamara, but we

fell in love with each other at the wrong time, really. I suppose instead of getting engaged last week, we should have decided to turn our love off for a couple of years, like punching a light switch, and then when it was more convenient, turning it back on again. Would you like that?"

"No, no!" Tamara wailed. "I *want* to be engaged to you, but I just don't want to be engaged so terribly long, that's all."

"If I had my way," said Andy, pulling her closer to him, "I would marry you right this minute; I guess you know that, don't you?"

"Uh-huh," she murmured, burying her face against his shoulder.

"But you know I don't have any money," he went on. "If Mom hadn't insisted on giving me that money she saved, I wouldn't even be on campus next year, but as it is, I will be there, and you'll be there, and we'll just have to hang on."

twenty-three

They did hang on, all their junior year. Tamara made several trips to Lake Vermilion and came to seem more and more like a daughter of Andy's family. He went to Michigan at Thanksgiving to see her family. Tamara had two married sisters, living in other towns, each with two children; so the only one at home with her mother and father was her brother —a senior in high school.

It had been a generation since Tamara's family had lived on a reservation, so they differed a good deal from his own family, Andy found. Mrs. Jay had graduated from high school and had had one year at a state teacher's college before she married. She was a leader in town, active in the PTA and the League of Women Voters, and in addition, took care of the books for her husband's business. He managed a thriving farm-implement store for a man who lived in Marquette, and he was active in community affairs, too. It was easier for Andy to see, after a visit with them, why Tamara's background turned her to the city rather than the reservation.

Yet different though his background was, he seemed to fit into her home very well, enough so that Mrs. Jay took him aside one day when Tamara was downtown, and said,

"Andy, I expect you have already discovered that Tamara has a mind of her own?"

He remembered various incidents and smiled, assuring her that he had. Her mother laughed heartily and said,

"Her father insists she is just like me. He thinks I run the family, and the other night he said, 'If Andy doesn't watch out, Tamara's going to run him just like you run me. I see symptoms of it already, and they aren't even married yet.' Would you accept a bit of advice from one who knows Tamara pretty well?"

"That sounds a little strange, coming from her mother," Andy responded, "but any suggestions are welcome."

Mrs. Jay laughed again and said, "Don't misunderstand me; her dad and I both enjoy Tam, she's bright and full of zip, but sometimes she pushes harder than anyone should to get her own way. If that happens, just leave her alone. She'll come to herself in time!"

Suddenly his junior year was ended, and Andy was home for a week of vacation. Then he went back to the city to work at the Indian Center, not as a volunteer, but as a full-fledged paid staff member, working mostly with teen-aged boys. Tamara was in charge of girls' work for the summer, and they had a great time working together.

It wasn't easy to cope with either the boys or the girls, some of them already addicted to drugs or heavy drinkers, nearly alcoholics; jobs were scarce that summer, especially for the younger ones, so Andy worked hard looking for things to keep them busy. Several times he was asked to go along with Mike's activist group on expeditions to protest some injustice done to Indians. Once it was to pack the courtroom at a trial they considered unfair. Once it was to join a crowd going to the Dakotas to occupy some abandoned buildings on land white men had seized in violation of treaty rights. Another time it was a parade downtown, complete with Indian dress and banners.

"I can't go," Andy would say. "I guess what you're doing is very important, but you go and take care of it. I have to stay here and take care of what *I'm* being paid to take care of this summer. My work is important, too."

Mike usually left in a huff. "You're so damn serious about it all," he'd say. "You're wet-nursing those kids. What difference does it make who's with 'em as long as somebody's here? You can get a substitute."

"I think it matters a lot whether Andy's with them or not," Tamara objected one day. "Remember Fred Beaudoin? Who salvaged him? It was Andy Thunder."

"Time will tell," Andy said. "Mr. LeMon was the one who really did it. I just kind of stood by and watched, you know. I think it takes a real pro to tackle some of the problems we're struggling with here. We ought to be able to make a lot more referrals than we do."

"Well, I agree with you about some of the hard-core cases," Tamara said, "but Andy, the general run of kids aren't alcoholics or drug addicts or anything too serious. They're poor, and lots of them come from one-parent homes. They don't do well in school because there's no one to help them. We can help that kind."

"Probably some of 'em just feel rejected," Andy said thoughtfully, "because they're Indians. When I look back on the trouble I had that year I was out of school, I think that was what was wrong with me."

Mike looked at him curiously. "Don't you *still* feel rejected because you're an Indian?" he asked. "*I* sure do and most of my friends do, too."

Andy hesitated for a minute before he answered. He didn't want what he said to be misunderstood. "Sometimes," he said carefully, "but only sometimes. It depends on where I am and what kind of people I'm with. When I'm with some white people, I feel just as comfortable as I do sitting here with you and Tamara; but with others I feel uneasy and out of place."

"Well," said Mike, "I can't honestly say that I feel accepted by any of 'em."

Tamara looked slightly shocked,

"You mean you don't feel comfortable when Angie is working here?" she asked. "And you don't like Marty?"

"That's exactly what I mean," Mike agreed. "Oh, don't get me wrong. Now you're twisting what I said around the wrong way. I *like* both of 'em all right, but I don't *trust* 'em, see? When the chips are down, if anything went wrong here, I think whites would stick up for whites every time and us Indians could go to hell."

"In other words, Mike," Andy said, quietly, "you don't trust me because I happen to have white friends?"

"No, I don't feel that way about you and Tam. I like you both, man, you know that, and I trust you, you're Indians. But I don't mind tellin' you that a whole bunch of my friends

185

sure get riled about you and your white pals." Mike was warming to his subject now. "I tell 'em it's your own business if you want to be chummy with whites, but they don't think so. And word's got out that there's a white teacher up at Vermilion who bosses you around. That's what sticks in their crops more than anything about you, I guess."

"You must mean Bob Underhill. He never bossed Andy around," Tamara flared.

"When did you meet Bob?" Andy asked, trying to sound innocent. "I didn't realize you and your friends were acquainted with him."

"Well, I never *have* met him, and neither have any of the boys," Mike said reluctantly. "I don't know what to think about you, Andy. You and me have always gotten along great, but when you won't go out with my bunch and show the white man that we've had it and we aren't gonna take any more of his guff, what can I say when the guys call you a 'white Indian'?"

"Don't say anything, Mike," Andy returned calmly. "I do my thing, and they do theirs. But I wouldn't go around knocking a white man you've never seen. Seems like your racism's hanging out when you do that!"

"What d'you mean, *'my racism'?*" Mike demanded.

Tamara started to reply, but Andy put up his hand to stop her.

"Let me answer," he said. "You mean, Mike, that you've never thought of a black or an Indian as being racist!"

"How do you mean we're racist?" Mike asked, more quietly.

"Well, if I'm going to be suspect with your friends because I happen to include several white people in my group of friends, aren't you being just as racist as whites who lump all Indians together as shiftless, dirty, lazy, thieving, drunken bums?"

There was a long pause while Mike thought. Finally he said, slowly,

"I suppose so, if you put it that way. I hadn't thought of that before, and if I think of it too long, it will probably wind up changing my whole life."

Suddenly they were all laughing. "Wouldn't it be horrible," Tamara giggled "if you were to get to trusting somebody who wasn't Indian?"

Andy was still smiling, but his eyes were serious as he said,

"Why don't you give it a try, man, and start with Angela and Marty? I'd hate to have you get chummy with the wrong kind and make a liar out of me right away!"

It was an exciting summer, with its good days and its bad days. There was the time that Stephanie Williams ran away. Stephanie was the lonely teenager who came to the Center almost every night and followed at Tamara's heels like a little lost puppy. She'd been reared on the Red Lake Reservation until her mother married a city man and moved her children to town. Stephanie was so homesick for her grandfather and grandmother that she couldn't stand it any longer and started to hitchhike back home. Andy and Mike caught up with her not far from the city limits just as she was about to get into a car with several men. They took her back to the Center where her frantic mother was waiting with Tamara. They all sat down for a talk about Stephanie's problem, and it ended with a plan for her to ride up to Red

Lake with Mike who was going to drive his parents up for the big Fourth of July celebration they had there every year.

The affair with Hank Green didn't have such a happy ending. Hank gave the Center trouble all summer; finally it reached a climax when he helped two older boys break into the office late one night after the Center was closed. It came out at the Juvenile Court hearing that he had known which window had a broken lock and had directed the boys to it. Hank had been outside standing guard while the petty cashbox was rifled and the boys got away to use the money for drugs. Andy went to the hearing with him and hoped to get him off with probation because he was so young; but it was refused. He was sent off to Red Wing Reformatory because this was his third similar offense and he had been on probation for a year.

But then, to take the bad taste of that disaster out of their mouths, there was Joey, a fatherless little waif, skinny and undernourished, terribly in need of a man in his life. At a staff meeting one day late in the summer it was decided that Tamara should call Big Brothers to see if one could be found for him. She came back from the phone to report that there was none available; the agency was swamped with calls and had a long waiting list of boys who needed just what Joey needed. Marty heard the story and volunteered to take Joey on for the few weeks left before summer session was over and he left for a visit home. The two took to each other immediately, and three weeks later when Marty drove around to the Center to say goodbye, Joey was sitting in the seat beside him.

"Where do you think *you're* going, Joey?" Mike asked, although everyone on the staff had known about Joey's vacation for several days.

"Don't you *know?*" the boy cried excitedly. "I'm going home with Marty. His mom asked my mom if I could, and I can. I'm going to see Chicago, too; it's a *huge* city. I'll be back for school, though. Marty and me's gonna do arithmetic together. He's not very good at it neither."

Andy, Tamara and Mike waved them off, and Mike was smiling as they walked back into the building,

twenty-four

Summer was gone all too soon. Andy's senior year began with a rush, and soon he found autumn fading into gray, freezing November. Then it was Christmas again. Angie and Marty came back from the holidays to announce their engagement at a party for their friends up in Andy's Tower. They planned a wedding in the summer as soon as school was out.

Winter term was a milestone in Andy's life. At last, after doing practice teaching in a suburban high school fall term, he was going to North High School in the city to teach under Jerry Eagle. In addition to teaching, Andy was anxious to see what this young Indian teacher he had heard about again and again was doing with a group of students that called themselves ILOA, Indian Leaders of America. Jerry invited him to meet with ILOA whenever he had time. From those sessions Andy learned how lonely some of those young Indians were, how left out of the white students' world, how afraid to face their futures. His contact with them deepened his interest in that special age group.

In the middle of his senior year, Andy had come face to face with his own future. Secondary school jobs were hard to come by that year, and all of his friends in the College of Ed. were in a lather. But for Andy, it was quite different. Opportunities were opening up for him at a dizzying rate. Jerry explained that it was because well-trained Indian high-school teachers were in demand, especially in the cities with large Indian populations.

"I agree with Tamara," he said to Andy. "Forget about your small-town idea. The city needs you,"

Most of the offers he had were good, and although he was more sophisticated about money than he once had been, the salaries sounded like a fortune. Offers came from as far away as Duluth, Rochester and Bismarck, North Dakota. He had chances to do everything from coaching track to teaching history in the Twin Cities and their suburbs. But still he put off the decision, although he knew he shouldn't wait much longer. Tamara was growing impatient, and he couldn't blame her; she was having job interviews, too, and her own choice depended to some extent on his. If he felt he ought to take a job in Bismarck, she certainly might want to think twice about heading up social service in a Minneapolis Indian center.

"Andy, what in heaven's name are you waiting for?" she demanded one day. "You've had fabulous offers. What do you want, the moon with a fence around it?"

They were sitting alone in the Tower looking out over the city. Earlier, others had been there, too, and they had all talked about the future. One of the girls had spoken a bit wistfully of years gone by when a girl could marry and settle down to keep house without Woman's Lib peering over her shoulder.

"Well gee, Karen," one of the men had said, "there's an easy way to fix that. Get pregnant right away, and nobody'll criticize!"

"Oh sure, somebody would. There's always some character around to carp about the population explosion," someone else said.

Everybody had laughed except Tamara. "I'm getting married next summer, too," she had responded crisply, "but I certainly don't intend to get pregnant right away."

"What, no babies in your future?" somebody teased. "You must be for minus population growth!"

"Sure there're babies in my future," Tamara had answered, "but with plenty of emphasis on *future!*"

Andy's mind jumped back to her remarks now as they sat there alone. He didn't know why her reply had offended him, but it had. Perhaps it was that she had said it so flippantly. At any rate, he was in a down mood, and she must have sensed it. She put down her coffee cup and snuggled close to him on the window seat. He put his arm around her, but it was mechanical. She pulled back so she could look at his face.

"Why Andy!" she exclaimed. "You're not happy with me, are you? You're cross!"

He shifted impatiently. "I'm not cross, Tamara," he said, really feeling angry with himself rather than with her. It was stupid to be irritated because she had said something that he agreed with, after all.

"Well, if you aren't cross you certainly *look* cross," she insisted. "What's the matter with you anyway? How come you didn't mention that job offer you got yesterday when everybody else was talking about jobs?"

"You mean the high school in St. Paul?" he asked. "How crazy can they be? Me teach *math*? They didn't even bother to check my major, evidently."

"What if they didn't?" Tamara answered. "I think it was quite an honor to be wanted by a big metropolitan high school, anyhow."

"Well," said Andy, "if you really want to know, I'm not ready to talk about any offer yet. I don't intend to go blabbing all over campus about every one I get. I'll wait until I'm good and ready to make up my mind, and then I'll tell people what I'm going to do."

When she answered him, her voice was tight and high.

"In other words, Andy, you mean that it's none of my business, don't you?"

"I don't mean any such thing," he snapped. "Don't be *dumb*, Tamara! You know perfectly well what I mean. I don't intend to go spreading all over what's our business, and *only* our business! And I don't want you blabbing, either, understand?"

This was the first time they had really quarreled. And one glimpse of the fury that flashed in Tamara's black eyes told him that he had gone too far. He reached out for her, but she whirled away from him and ran to the door, snatching her jacket as she ran.

"I'm going home," she announced, her voice high and unfamiliar. "Don't bother to come."

193

"Of course I'm coming," he shot back, following her down the narrow, winding stairs. "Do you think I'd let you walk home alone this time of night?"

"I certainly do, Andrew Thunder, after the things you have just said to me," she answered, and slammed out the door.

He had to run to catch up with her, and she walked three steps in front of him all four blocks to the house where she lived. He left her at the door, and she stalked in without a word or a backward glance. He knew he should have followed her, and told her how sorry he was for everything; but he couldn't yet, and besides, she probably would have slapped his face!

He walked back home, seething alternately with anger and remorse; but by the time he got up his stairs the anger had dwindled away, leaving only the remorse. He sat down and tried to analyze what had happened. He realized, thinking it over more or less calmly, that he had *wanted* her to get angry. It satisfied some kind of need in him, but now that it had happened, he was so shaken that he had to do something.

He remembered being told by his mother never to sleep on anger. So he rushed down the stairs and out to the phone booth on the corner, amazed at the way his hand shook as he dialed her number. It was late, but a sleepy voice answered the ring and in a moment Tamara came; he felt sure she must have been awake, waiting for his call.

"Hello," she said, and her voice was thick with tears.

"Tamara, if I come over will you come to the door?"

"Oh Andy!" she couldn't say any more, she didn't need to.

He hung up without waiting for more and raced the four blocks to her house. She was waiting and threw open the door as he ran up the steps. She was in his arms and crying. Neither one of them slept on anger that night, but this had been a frightening experience for both of them, and neither forgot it.

"I believe it was good therapy," said Tamara, thoughtfully, as they walked one evening. "I think I really love you better than I ever did before."

Andy was trying to sort out his own thoughts as he listened to her.

Finally he spoke carefully, "I don't believe I love you any *better* than I did before; I've loved you as much as it's possible for me to love since we were sophomores, at least. But I feel a little different about it, I guess. Maybe we've been exploring deeper into our feelings. Probably we used to take each other too much for granted, do you see what I mean? It was more on the surface of our lives."

"Yes!" she exclaimed eagerly. "That's a better way to put it. I think you mean that we met, fell in love, you proposed, I accepted, and we just expected everything to go along smoothly. We'd get jobs and get married. Nothing to it. Then we'd have babies, they'd grow up and have babies, and we'd all live happily ever after. We didn't believe anything could happen to damage our being together."

"That's just about what I had in mind," Andy agreed, "and then all of a sudden, pffft! In just a few words the whole thing almost blew up in our faces. Every time I think how easy it would be for us to lose each other, I get cold chills."

"I know," Tamara nodded soberly, "so do I, but we've learned a lesson, haven't we? That's what I was clumsily trying to say about its being good therapy. You really do think we've learned a lesson, don't you?"

He took both of her hands and turned her so that he could look straight into her eyes.

"I hope we have, Tamara," he said slowly. "But before we decide where we're going to work next year, something's got to give between us. Until that's settled, I don't think we're going to know how much of a lesson we've learned, or how strong our love for each other really is."

She buried her face on his shoulder and was quiet for a moment, and then she murmured, almost too softly to be heard,

"I couldn't bear to lose you, Andy!"

April warmed into May, and still he dillydallied until one day a letter came from the superintendent of schools in his own town. Mr. Olson's letter was apologetic; he knew it was very late to approach Andy about a teaching position for next year, but his teachers had all been hanging onto their jobs like glue. He hadn't expected any turnover at all until yesterday when one of his teachers resigned to accept a position in his hometown in Iowa.

Could Andy come, or had he already taken one of the offers Bob said he had had? Mr. Olson said he couldn't offer a magnificent starting salary, or even a great number of Indian students. There might not be more than a half-dozen next fall, but those few could really be helped by an Indian teacher on the faculty. Besides that, he and Bob both felt the white students needed Andy almost as much as the Indians.

It was an exciting letter, a warm letter; and it was, Andy realized, what he had been waiting for.

He'd scarcely finished reading it when Tamara came rushing up the Tower steps to say that Bob had called from school and wanted Andy to call him back as soon as he could. It had nothing to do with the family, no one was sick. But she had no idea what he wanted.

"I have an idea what's on his mind," Andy said. "Read this."

She took the letter and sat down on the couch to read it while Andy put on socks and loafers and got ready to walk back with her. He didn't have a telephone, so people had to call him at her house. He watched her face as she read and marveled at how quickly it registered her feelings. He could tell exactly what was passing through her mind: first, surprise; then shock; and finally a mixture of fear and exasperation.

"Andy, you wouldn't!" she exclaimed. "How could that man have the nerve even to suggest it? I can't imagine Bob's encouraging him to think there's the slightest chance of your going way up in the north woods to teach. He shouldn't have!"

"Don't blame Bob," Andy said defensively. "He's only thinking about how badly an Indian teacher is needed up there."

"Well," she flared, "he should know better. It's selfish of him. You've developed a real interest in urban Indian problems, and besides," she finished, "you've got *me* and my career to consider *now*. Don't forget that."

"I won't," he promised somberly. "I haven't forgotten that

for a minute, Tamara. But this is what I've been waiting for. You wondered what was holding me up. Well, this was it. I had to weigh this one against all the others. Now we're right smack up against it, just the way I knew we'd be, and it's going to be tough."

"It certainly is!" she fired back.

They walked to her house in complete silence, each one wrapped in his own thoughts. She sat on the step in the front hall while he dialed the numbers and waited, hoping Bob would answer. He did.

"Did you get Mr. Olson's letter?" he asked eagerly.

Andy said he had, and Tamara had just finished reading it, but she didn't think much of it. Bob chuckled and said,

"Well, I hardly thought she would, but maybe she'll change her mind when she hears some news I have for both of you. Just today Mr. Olson got word from Washington that federal funding for a new project is coming through after all. We'd about given up on it. I didn't tell you it was in the wind for fear it would fizzle, but we've been working on the idea for a year. We decided that I should call you and ask you to come and bring Tamara as soon as you can, because she's involved, too."

"Give me some notion what you're talking about," Andy pleaded. "Mr. Olson didn't say anything in the letter about my coming up."

"I can't tell you over the phone," Bob said. "It's too long a story. Could you two possibly get away for a couple of days? Mr. Olson needs to sit down with you and have a good interview."

"Just a minute."

Andy covered the mouthpiece with his hand and told Tamara what Bob suggested. How about it? It was a warm spring day, but her voice was as cold as ice when she said,

"Tell Bob for me that I appreciate the thought, but no thanks. I wouldn't think of leaving campus on a wild goose chase with graduation less than a month away."

The ice melted to white heat after she heard Andy tell Bob he'd be there the next day on the noon bus. He hung up and turned to her. Her eyes were shooting sparks when she cried out to him in fury,

"Andy Thunder, have you taken leave of your senses?"

"No," he answered as calmly as he could, trying to hang onto himself this time, "but it looks to me as though you're about to take leave of yours!"

twenty-five

Andy went home alone the next morning. Bob met the bus at noon and took him to his house for lunch with Ann and Mr. Olson. There Andy heard that some of the federal money set apart to improve Indian education was going to be used for something that was really special.

Their high school had been chosen as a center to which Indian students from all over the area would be taken by bus. There would be special classes on Indian culture, there would be tutors to help students who were behind in the basic subjects, and best of all, there would be a trained social worker to help with problems both at school and at home with parents.

"So now you see what I had in mind when I told you over the phone that this involved Tamara, too," said Bob.

"I was disappointed that she couldn't come with you," Mr. Olson broke in, "because I wanted to talk to you both about this. It seems such a natural to have Tamara for our social worker and you for the teacher in charge of the project. One of the first stipulations is that those two key people must be Indian."

After Bob went back to his afternoon class, Andy and Mr. Olson sat in the Underhills' living room and discussed details of the job, until the superintendent finally said,

"How about it, Andy? Sound good to you? I'd certainly like to get your name on a contract before you go back to the city!"

Andy sat in silence, so Mr. Olson went into the kitchen to talk to Ann and get a refill on coffee. Andy's reverie took him back to the city streets where he had seen so many young Indians, just off the reservations. Most of them had been down on their luck because there was no way to earn a living at home, they were school dropouts with no trade, resentful of BIA paternalism. After awhile they'd had it and went off to the city to get a job.

It all seemed so glamorous. But then the money began to dwindle, and it was time to look for a job; but there weren't jobs, not even for the Indians who had lived there for a long time, let alone for the new ones without any job record and references. Suddenly it was just like the reservation, but in the city they didn't have their families or even the hateful BIA to fall back on. After that it was welfare and the cheap bars and a ride home with an Indian Patrol team like Mike and Andy if they were lucky. What an ugly circle!

What if there had been an Indian teacher on the reservation, or in the little town where they went to school, to help them along so they didn't drop out at sixteen? Such a teacher could prepare them for living, wherever they decided to go. The circle didn't need to be so ugly.

201

"How about it, Andy?"

Mr. Olson had returned and was smiling at him expectantly. But Andy heard not only Mr. Olson, but Tamara, too, angry and pleading all at the same time, ". . . you've got me to consider now."

Andy was sure Mr. Olson would think he was an indecisive goon who didn't know his own mind, but still he hesitated. Mr. Olson studied his face briefly and then said, almost as though he had read his mind,

"I shouldn't expect you to make a decision this important without your girl here with you. Go back to the U. and talk it over with her and let me know as soon as you can, eh? I'll keep both jobs open for you until I hear."

Andy thanked him, and the two rode over to school together: Bob's one o'clock class was leaving as Andy arrived, and Bob was busy putting new algebra problems on the board. He waggled his finger in greeting and hurried on. Andy slipped into a back seat, and in a moment the kids began to file in, looking at him curiously. They were no more nor less interesting to him than the youngsters he had had in practice teaching. They all looked alike, blue jeans, T-shirts, long hair, sneakers.

Just as the bell rang the last one slipped through the door, an Indian boy dressed like all the rest, but his face was different. It wasn't the copper color and the high, wide cheekbones that made it seem different. It was the sullen, turned-down mouth and the blank look, and the most lackluster eyes Andy had ever seen. The boy slid into his seat and looked furtively around to see if he was going to be called for tardiness. Nobody had noticed him; nobody paid any attention. For a fleeting instant a faint expression of relief crossed his face, and then it went blank again and he stared at the blackboard with eyes that Andy doubted saw a thing.

Andy shifted in his chair, the boy heard the sound and jerked around to look at him. He saw Andy's copper skin and black hair, and the boy's black eyes met Andy's own black eyes. The transfiguration that took place was blinding. The lackluster eyes lit up as though a flame had been kindled in back of them, bringing the whole dead face to life. It was over in an instant, but it lasted long enough for Andy to make a decision.

Without a moment's hesitation he walked out the back door of Bob's math class and down the hall to the office. Mr. Olson was busy with papers on his desk when Andy walked in, but he got up and came to meet him. He must have seen something different in Andy's bearing, but he waited for Andy to speak.

"Will it take long to get a contract ready for me to sign?" Andy asked abruptly.

"No longer than it takes to type your name in the right place on the form," Mr. Olson replied.

He took a printed form from a drawer and screwed it into the typewriter, tapped out Andy's name in a blank space, and motioned for him to sit in the chair beside his desk. Andy read the contract automatically and took out his pen. Mr. Olson laid a detaining hand on his arm.

"Just a minute, Andy," he said soberly, "much as I want that signature, I want even more to be sure that this sudden decision isn't an impulse. We don't want any regrets, later."

"Thank you, but this isn't an impulse," Andy assured him.

"As a matter of fact, I guess I made this decision a long time ago. I simply had it confirmed ten minutes back."

"All right." Mr. Olson nodded, and said nothing more until Andy had signed his name and they had shaken hands. Then he said,

"D'you mind telling me what happened to make you come in here like this? Less than an hour ago I got the distinct impression you weren't about to commit yourself, maybe because your girl wasn't enthusiastic about coming away up here to the wilderness."

Andy hesitated a moment, but finally decided that he might as well be honest with Mr. Olson.

"Well," he began, fingering the contract in his pocket, "actually she isn't. But not because she has anything against the North country," he added hastily, defending Tamara. "It's just that she feels she has to do her thing in the city among city Indians. She's been working with children and old folks there ever since she was a freshman, and she's so tied up with them and their problems, you'd never believe it. She thinks they need us more than the reservation Indians do. She's terribly committed to her work."

Mr. Olson nodded. "Yes, Bob told me."

"She's the greatest as far as I'm concerned" Andy said. "But she can't seem to understand why I want to come up to this part of the state where there aren't nearly so many Indians, when I could teach in the city and do so much more good."

"You don't see it that way," said the superintendent thoughtfully.

"No, I don't," Andy answered. "I want to do something

like preventive medicine, I guess." He was fumbling for the right words to express how he felt. "An Indian friend I work with on an Indian Patrol at night uses those two words to describe what we do when we pick up Indians in trouble and take them home."

He stopped abruptly, wondering if he was boring Mr. Olson, but evidently he wasn't.

"Let's face it," Andy continued. "Most young Indians on the reservations are going to wind up in a city somewhere because they can't earn a decent living at home. If they hate school and drop out, as I did once upon a time, they're going to end in the gutter, a lot of them. I'd like to try to prevent that up here rather than attempt to cure the disease once they've gotten sick and disillusioned in the cities."

"You're probably right, Andy," Mr. Olson commented.

"I'm sure I am, Mr. Olson!" Andy exclaimed. "Take Bob Underhill; much as I love that guy, I don't believe he can do for every Indian what an Indian teacher could, and Bob would be the first to admit it. Do you understand what I mean? I'd trust Bob or Ann with my life, but lots of Indians wouldn't."

"I understand exactly," said Mr. Olson, gently. "You're trying to tell me that hardly any Indians trust white people, and I've learned that, to my sorrow. That's why I want you and Tamara both for this job up here. But you still haven't told me what sent you here in such a hurry to sign a contract."

"I saw an Indian boy," Andy said. "He saw me and caught fire for just an instant. I thought if I were here next year, I might rekindle the flame and keep it going."

Mr. Olson cleared his throat and said quietly,

"I know the boy. Even Bob hasn't been able to turn him on; but might it cost you your marriage?"

"I'm afraid it might," was Andy's reply. "I have to come here. I know that now. But Tamara has a right to make up her own mind about what's right for her."

twenty-six

When Andy had told Mr. Olson that Tamara might not be willing to come north to work, he hadn't really believed what he was saying. How could she possibly miss seeing what a great opportunity they were getting? Even thinking about her saying no was so painful that he pushed the idea as far away as he could. Until he handed his contract to Tamara that night and saw the look on her face, he wasn't able to accept what should have been apparent to him all along.

She handed it back to him and sat in silence on the step of her house. When she finally spoke, there was no anger in her voice, nor even an icy aloofness. He heard only weariness and grief, as though she had spent hours while he was away thinking about their problem and had come at last to believe there was no way out for them.

"I had the feeling that they would talk you into it," she said. "While you were gone, I went over our situation in my mind. At first I thought I had made a mistake, not going

207

with you. I might have been able to keep you from doing this, but then I decided it was better this way. It would have been trading on our love, and that's no good, Andy."

What love? he thought bitterly, but he stifled the impulse to say it out loud. Instead he tried to keep his voice low and quiet to match her control.

"Tamara, nobody talked me into anything," he protested. "Mr. Olson was very understanding. Even after I had decided to sign the contract and asked him for it, he suggested that I shouldn't be in a hurry, that maybe I should wait until I had talked it all over with you again."

"Well then, why *did* you sign it?" Tamara asked.

"I saw an Indian boy," he told her, eagerly, "and if I hadn't any more reasons, just that one—"

"Just one Indian boy!" Tamara interrupted impatiently. "Just *one Indian boy!* Andy Thunder, I can't believe you know what you're saying. One boy, and you go overboard when there are dozens of them in this city."

"*Wait a minute,* Tamara," he begged, "you didn't give me a chance to tell about him. He wasn't just any Indian boy. Let me tell you."

He hurried on to explain, but he could see that he wasn't getting to her. She was looking at him but she didn't see him. At least she was letting him talk, so he rushed on about the new project, about the exciting plan for them to work together as a team, teacher and social worker. He knew this was his trump card; if this didn't change her thinking, nothing could.

When he finished, he sat expectantly, waiting for her to react. He had been as persuasive as he knew how to be. If she wouldn't rise to this chance for them to work together, he didn't have anything else to say. She did react, but he wondered if she had heard a word he said.

"Andy, we're about as far apart as we could be on this, aren't we?" she began. "Every time we talk about it, I see it. We agree on only one thing: each of us must serve our own people. But you think you can't do your thing except in the northland, and I think I can't do mine except in the slums of the cities."

He tried once more. "But Tamara, don't you think you could be happy up there with me? With our two salaries we'd have enough money to buy a little house in town or maybe even build one on the Vermilion Reservation." He was pleading with her now. "Don't you think that in time you could realize that by helping Indians up there, you'd be solving some of the city problems, too?"

Suddenly Tamara was on her feet, eyes flashing, copper cheeks flaming deep red.

"No, I don't—all I realize is that you've signed a contract to teach in that God-forsaken wilderness, when you knew how I feel about it. Do you think I'm willing to be just an old-time squaw who follows her man anywhere he wants to go? Well, I can tell you something; you've got the wrong girl!"

"No," Andy answered, his own voice rising, "I don't think that, and I wouldn't want you to be that kind of a wife, but I certainly did think our love meant enough to you that you'd at least *talk* to Mr. Olson."

"Oh you did?" cried Tamara. "Well, I can tell you *I* have some questions in my own mind about our so-called love.

How about all the great opportunities you've turned your back on here in the cities? I'm beginning to think we'd better make a clean break now; I don't think we should see each other again. Let's end our University days at peace with ourselves, at least!"

"My God, Tamara, don't you love me at *all?*" he exploded.

"Of course I *love* you. I'll *always* love you," she cried. "But I don't want to talk about it *anymore*. We just go round and round in circles. Go on away and leave me alone. Go on home now, and don't ever come back!"

He went, but he did try to see her. She was never at home. He telephoned, but she never answered. He waited for her after her classes, but she always seemed to slip out without his seeing her. Finally, he decided to write to Mother and Johnny, and to Bob and Ann and tell them the engagement was broken—there would be no wedding. He wrote long letters, explaining all about it so he wouldn't need to discuss it with them when he got home. He also told them not to come down for commencement as they were planning because he simply couldn't go through with it. He would ask to have his diploma mailed, and he'd be home as soon as he could clear out the apartment and pack things up, after his classes were over.

Marty was his pillar of strength those final weeks. He came over with his books and they studied together; sometimes they just sat in silence. Once Andy lashed out about Tamara to him, but more often he lectured himself for being a "damn fool," and Marty would listen. That was all Andy wanted—someone he cared about to let him talk on and on when he felt like it. Several times Marty said to Andy,

"Hold everything, I don't believe this is the end for you and Tamara."

But Andy thought it was. Obviously she didn't even intend to see him again. The end of the term came, and he packed his things, cleaned up the Tower as well as he could, and got ready to leave. He had the ordeal of saying goodbye to all his Indian friends at the Center. It had been hard to explain why he and Tamara didn't come there together anymore and why they had decided to call off the summer wedding that everyone had expected. Stephanie Williams had been especially upset, and Mike, of course. Andy felt at the end that he owed Mike more than just the casual explanation he had given. So he told him the whole miserable story as briefly as he could, and Mike's reaction was some small comfort to him.

"Gee, but I'm sorry, Andy," Mike said. "It seemed to me that you and Tam were just made for each other, but I think you did right. Sure we need guys like you here in town, but when I go up to Red Lake to visit our relatives, I see that the kids on the reservations need Indian teachers *bad*. And when it comes right down to the crunch, a fellow has to do what he thinks is right for him, doesn't he?"

Strangely, Andy found himself saying to Mike, "Yeah, and I guess a girl does, too."

Mother Beaudoin and Fred heard the whole story, too. They were heartbroken, but both of them said, echoing Marty's feelings,

"You and Tamara'll get back together again, someday."

The last goodbye to the Tower was even harder than Andy had expected. Everything there reminded him of Tamara, for many of the things that had made it homelike belonged to her. He packed them in a box, a couple of sofa pillows, a picture, a small lamp, and carried them over to her house, but she was gone—not just temporarily out, but *gone*.

"I don't know where she went," her roommate said. "I wasn't here when she left; it must have been sudden because yesterday morning when I went out she didn't say a word about going anywhere, and when I came home last night she was gone. She's scarcely talked to anybody, Andy, since you broke up. I'm really worried about her. She hardly eats a thing, and she's gotten so thin. You should see her."

"I've tried; believe me, I've tried!" Andy said dryly.

"Oh, I know," her roommate assured him. "I've seen you at the door. I'm sorry, Andy. I'm sure she really loves you!"

"Thanks," Andy responded. "I wish I could be sure of that!"

He lugged the box back to his house and put it with the boxes of books to be sent home United Parcel. Then he took his suitcase and caught the bus.

twenty-seven

Bob was waiting at the bus stop for Andy when he arrived after his long, dreary bus ride.

"Shall we just go right on out to your house?" he asked cheerfully, putting Andy's suitcase in the trunk and starting the motor.

"No, I don't think so," Andy said. "I feel like walking down to the lake for a few minutes, do you mind?"

"Not at all," Bob assured him. "Probably be better that way. I've just thought of a phone call I promised to make, and I'll tell Ann you're home and that you'll have supper with us before we go out to the village. OK?"

"Swell," Andy answered, trying to be cheerful, too.

Bob drove off down the street, and Andy walked through town to the tiny East Two River and picked his way along its timbered edge as he had that day so long before when he had come home from lumber camp. It was the same kind of day, soundless, the little boathouses still locked up, waiting for the summer people to come. He came at last to the grassy knoll where the gaunt old tower had once stood. He walked across and down the other side to the shore. There was the place where he had found his boat. He heard a motor faintly over the other side of Whisky Island. Somebody was out on the lake, probably fishing. It would be good to fish again.

The boat was coming closer; in a minute it would round the rocky shore of Whisky, and he could see it. Maybe it was someone he knew. It was coming around now, and Andy couldn't believe what he saw. It couldn't possibly be anything but a mirage. He had been thinking about *Josie's Coat,* so he thought this boat coming toward him across the water was his. Someone was out in his boat. The little ten-horse, missing now and then the way *Josie's* did, was driving it closer to him, and he could see at last that it was *Josie's Coat.*

Josie was running a little crooked, the way she always did. But who could be running the boat? It wasn't near enough yet for him to see, against the pale blue of the spring sky. Maybe Johnny had taken it out, or maybe Harry was home for the summer. No, it was a girl with long black hair. Mother never let Ellen and Rosemary take it out. Who had his boat? It was coming closer now so he could see the girl clearly. She was waving and calling. He could hear her voice above the clamor of the motor.

"Andy, Andy!"

It was Tamara. What was she doing here? The last few minutes of waiting before the boat eased into shore were an agony. But then Tamara was standing up in the shaky old craft, reaching her arms out to him. He lifted her out and hauled *Josie's Coat* up on the narrow strip of sand; then he pulled Tamara down beside him on the grass.

"Tamara, where did you come from?" he demanded. "What were you doing on Lake Vermilion in *Josie's Coat?*"

They were such mundane, stupid things to say to her when he could hardly speak for the choke in his throat. Tears were streaming down her face.

"I've been waiting for you, Andy. Why didn't you come? What took you so long?" she cried.

"Tamara, how did you know I was walking down to the lake? Only Bob knew."

"That was easy," she answered. "Bob called to say you were on your way down East Two River. I jumped into the boat and here I am. She never went so fast; she must have known you were coming! I love her so much; we'll keep her always, won't we?"

Andy tipped her face up to his and said the words he'd been trying to say to her all those nightmare days,

"Tamara, I'm going to tear up that contract of mine. We'll be married as soon as we can get a license, and we'll go back to the city right away so I can see if one of those teaching jobs is still—"

His words were muffled by her hand over his mouth.

"Oh no we won't," she said, pressing closer into the curve of his arm. "We'll be married, of course. How long does it take to get a license? But the contract part—you can't do that. It's much too late now, because you see, *I've* signed a contract, too, and I don't think Mr. Olson would like it much if both of us tore up our contracts!"

Andy's head was swimming. "Tamara, for heaven's sake what happened to change your mind?"

Even as he asked, certain words were beginning to take form in his mind. He hadn't thought of them for more than a year; perhaps if he had remembered them sooner—! What was it Tamara's mother had said to him? "If she get's too determined, leave her alone. She'll find herself in time!"

Tamara smiled. "Well," she said, "I'd love to say that it was all my own smartness, but it really wasn't. Let's start back to the village, and I'll tell you. Your mother and Johnny are waiting."

So they got into *Josie's Coat* and while she carried them crookedly back across the bay, Tamara shouted above the noise of the motor. From the very night that they had broken their engagement, Tamara had been miserably unhappy. She had spent hours alone, trying to straighten out her feelings, and had finally decided it was all her fault and there must be *some* way out for two people who really loved each other.

"But I've always been so proud and stiff-necked about things," said Tamara contritely. "I can hardly ever say I'm sorry."

Just as she had made up her mind to look up Andy and ask his forgiveness, Bob and Ann arrived at her door one evening. They were so upset by Andy's letter that they had driven in to see her on the spur of the moment. When she heard that they knew all about it, of course she began to cry and insist that it had been all her fault and she was getting ready to tell Andy so.

At that point Andy interrupted to insist that it was all his fault for being so stubborn and mulish about where he taught school; it wasn't important enough to ruin their lives over. But Tamara shushed him and went on to say that Bob asked

her why she wasn't interested in the wonderful new govern-
ment-funded plan for Indian students in their school.

She had to admit to him that she had been so mad at Andy
when he tried to tell her about it that she hadn't heard half
of what he was saying. So Bob had gone over the whole
thing again, and finally said,

"Mr. Olson is still interested in getting you and Andy to
work together as a team. I'd suggest that you ride back with
us right now and let him tell you all about it, only if your engagement is really broken it might be a bit awkward."

Tamara giggled. "I told them that our engagement would
be put back together again just as soon as I had a chance to
talk to you, Andy, that is, if you'd have me!"

Andy let *Josie* steer herself around in a circle while he told
Tamara emphatically that he would!

"But you didn't go back with them, did you?" he asked.
"You still had more classes, didn't you?"

"One more," Tamara nodded, "but somehow it didn't seem
as important as talking to Mr. Olson, and besides, I already
knew I was getting an *A* in that one. Bob thought I ought to
come right away, even though Mr. Olson had promised to
wait for me. I was all for accepting the job then and there
with Bob as proxy, but he wanted me to be sure I knew
what I was doing. So Ann helped me pack. We threw
everything into my bags and put the overflow into boxes and
drove around to the Tower to tell you; but it was all dark, so
we set out for Lake Vermilion. It was 1:00 A.M. when we
got here!"

"You might have left me a note!" Andy exclaimed, half-
angry. "Nobody knew what had become of you."

"Oh my dearest, I know," she said remorsefully, "but we were so excited, and it was getting late, and we were so anxious to get back; so we just dashed off. I've hurt both of us so terribly because I was so bullheaded!"

"I don't want to hear any more of that, Tamara," Andy said. "You had just as much right to your opinion as I had to mine, but I'm so glad you want to come here!"

Josie was nosing the dock in front of the house, and Andy looked up to see his mother and Johnny waiting for them. Marty and Angela, hand in hand, were running down the hill, Bob and Ann were arriving with their children, and some of his brothers and sisters were racing out of the house.

"What's everybody doing here?" he shouted to Tamara above the racket of *Josie's* old motor.

"Well," she shouted back, "I guess they've come to celebrate our putting it all together again. Let's try to keep them for our wedding!"

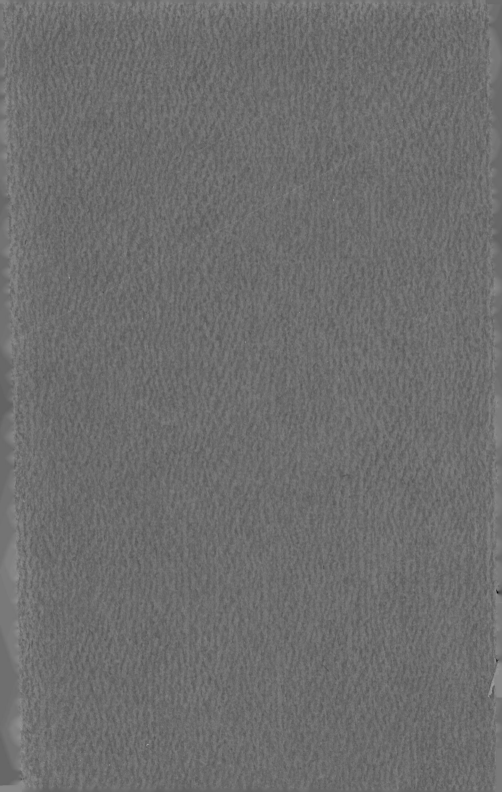